Bleeding rose

Katia Minch

Contents

Chapter ~One~

The black double vest fit annoyingly well. The silky cloth fit snugly over the white crisp dress shirt with the black tie tucked in. It made me wonder, not for the first time, how Kristy knew my size.

Speaking of the creeper, I thought, as she poked her head in the back room to check if I was ready.

"Hurry, table six is requesting you."

She tried to blind me with one of her dazzling smiles before turning away with a wave of her long blond braid.

I made sure the long sleeves on the dress shirt allowed the cuff to brush my palms before I stepped out to the front of the shop. As usual, the brightly lit café had half of the tables taken by the regular customers. Honestly, it was more of a mini restaurant then a café. Still, it was my living.

The Red Rose Café originally hired me to work in the kitchen. I was a decent cook, though Kristy told me otherwise. She would always steel the readied cake slices and cookies when she had a chance. Her grandmother would often scold her—Mrs. Clair was the owner.

One day, however, Mrs. Clair's nitwit of a daughter dragged me out from behind the kitchen. One of our newer customers, a woman in her late twenties, wanted to compliment whoever had baked the cake she feasted on. She took one look at me and for some reason dropped her plate. We were lucky I was able to catch it on time. Mrs. Clair and Kristy had an exchange of words before I was given a new uniform. The next day I had been "promoted" as they said, to a host that worked out front.

At first I seriously had no idea what I was doing. But the customers seemed to like me, and I stuck with it. After all, Mrs. Clair offered a higher pay. I needed the money.

Now, I walked over to table six where two girls in their teens waited. I recognize them—these two came every Saturday for the cake and hot chocolate. The majority of the regular visitors were people of the like, girls. I thought it was because of the relaxed and simple theme the café repre-sented, but when I started as a host and the amount of usual customers rose, Kristy had a different theory she wouldn't tell me.

"Hey Nathan." They greeted.

I smiled politely and tipped my head in greeting. "Good evening ladies." I took out the small note pad from the black cloth pouch that hung on my waist. "The usual?"

They giggled strangely and nodded.

I walked to the counter where Kristy was arranging the sweets and handed her the paper. "Is your fresh cake out yet?" She glanced at it, then at the girls at the table, and rolled her eyes. "What?" I asked.

"Why do they even order?"

"What?" She laughed and nibbled on a cookie before responding with a smirk, "They only order because you're serving them. They barely even eat what they pay for."

I frowned. I had no idea what she was talking about. She shook her head in defeat as she realized I was clueless. She disappeared behind the back and returned with two small plates with the pastry balanced in the middle. I nodded and walked it over to their tables.

"Enjoy your meal." I smiled like how Kristy taught—or forced, as I'd come to call it—me to.

Suddenly Kristy came bounding toward me as I walked behind the counter. "Someone reserved!"

The business was small, where not a lot of people knew about it. Our "regulars" were the people who heard about it from someone else and preferred our quiet shop compared to the louder, public ones. It was rare that someone in our ranks of customers would reserve the back room, a private table costing slightly more than three times the price of a whole pie.

"And you'll be leaving me out here to bus by myself while you get to waste your time and serve the back room?" I asked in mockery. I've never hosted for the reserved guests, mostly because I never wanted to. I preferred the front. Kristy would usually take the orders from the back. Plus, I'd probably make a fool of myself.

She shook her head, her green eyes bouncing wildly. "Nope, Grandma says it's your turn. They requested you."

My mockery disappeared. "Kristy, I really don't want to—"

"She said they give big tips."

Instantly I bit my lip and held my tongue. I needed the money. Kristy, as well as her grandmother, knew this well from when I would pitch in extra hours in the early morning before school. I sighed in defeat. "Fine."

She jumped up and down and poking me. Being the happy and hyper person she was, she began fretting over my hair. On instinct I jumped and shied away. She realized her mistake and held her hand to her mouth as her eyes went wide.

"Oh Nathan, I'm sorry. I forgot."

"It's okay." I muttered, shaking myself off.

She dutifully dropped the issue and tried to lighten the atmosphere by fingering the tray of cookies on the counter. "Don't expect those to be here when you're done with your shift."

I shoved a smile on my face and gave a small laugh. "Have fun managing all the tables."

She rolled her eyes and played with the end of her braid, a gesture you would always find her doing. "I doubt any of those girls will stay when I tell them you're working another table."

Yet again, I frowned, not comprehending what she was saying. She laughed un-lady like and shoved me toward the hall with a side door connecting to the kitchen and another to the back room. I heaved a great sigh and pulled my sleeves again down out of habit so it partly covered my hands.

I pushed open the door. The walls in the room were much like out in the front: a soft crimson coat. The table in the center was a standard oak but instead of the usually chairs, customers were granted with the high back seating. This room was made for comfort and privacy, usually reserved by families for birthdays and the likes. Considering it cost more, that meant I got paid more.

I looked at the two occupants. One of which I recognized. The middle-aged woman was Mrs. Kenneth. She came here often for coffee in the mornings.

"Good evening Mrs. Kenneth." I smiled widely. Kristy was right. I wasn't sure who she was or what this woman did, but she always left a generous tip. She was somewhat of a friend, though I've ever seen her outside the shop. Apparently she was my parent's friend, so she knew me since I was little.

"Nathan! I was hoping you were working today." She laughed and smiled.

I gave a short laugh. "I'm always working."

"How have you been?"

I shrugged. "Surviving."

She was a very polite woman and always happy. She had soft brown hair always seen in a loose bun and her bright eyes were ever happy. The few lines on her face did not do justice to her personality. She clapped her hands together once and motioned to her accompaniment.

"This is my son Ryder. Ryder, this is the Rose's best host, Nathan."

Her son spared me a glance and observed with a near sneer on his lips. Great attitude. He didn't say hello but rolled his similar gray eyes and crossed his arms, signaling his obvious annoyance.

My job was to be "charming and polite" as Kristy ordered. I wasn't sure what she meant when she added, "Though, little practice in the charming area is needed," but I made sure to always be polite.

"Pleasure to meet you Mr. Kenneth." I kept the smile on as I turned back to his mother. "What will you two have this evening?"

"Let's see..." Mrs. Kenneth looked at the menu and ordered coffee and something off the appetizer menu. She didn't wait for her son but ordered him an espresso and a slice of my chocolate mousse.

"Be right back." I nodded and left to the kitchen. When I passed Kristy and she asked who had reserved, I mouthed, "Kenneth."

She scrunched her nose and whined. "Lucky."

I went to the back and cut a piece of the cake and made the drinks as well as the appetizer bread. I placed all of the contents on a tray and went to the back.

Before I opened the door, I thought I heard the two arguing. "You have to bring your grades up."

"It doesn't matter mom." The boy grumbled.

"Yes it does." There was a pause. "You're grounded until you bring your grades up."

"What?" Ryder's voice rose. "Damn it mom, that's not fair!"

I visibly winced when he swore and decided I should enter before it gets any more awkward. I poked my head in and announced, "Foods ready."

Mrs. Kenneth, who had been resting her head in her palm, snapped up and motioned for me to come in. One hand held the tray and the other set the table. When I was done I stood aside with the tray under my arm dutifully.

"So Nathan," Mrs. Kenneth started. I smiled at her to continue. "How are your grades?"

I wasn't sure what to say. "Well, my lowest is an A."

She nodded as if thinking something over. "Have you ever tutored someone?"

I had a sinking feeling I knew where this was going. "A couple of times before." I responded hesitantly.

Again her eyes lit up. "How would you feel about tutoring Ryder?"

"Mom!" He shouted.

She ignored him completely and focused on me. "I'm sorry, I don't have a lot of time, and the time I have is spent here working."

She dismissed this with a wave of her hand. "You'll be paid of course if you agree. You need the money right?"

I bit my lip. Considering she was my parent's friend, she knew my situation. On top of everything else, I was sure she often talked to Mrs. Clair.

"I don't know Mrs. Kenneth." I glanced at Ryder who was glaring at me through his peripheral vision.

She caught my glance and laughed. "Don't mind him. He's thrilled." She placed a hand on his arm, but I clearly saw the hard pinch she shared. "How's twenty dollars an hour, two hours, from Monday to Friday?"

Wait, that meant I'd get forty bucks a day, multiply that by five and that's two hundred a week. As amazing as that sounded, I was way to polite to be paid that much. Plus, I'd never had that much money before. It was out of my range. "I can not accept that much."

She frowned. "I thought you needed–"

"I do," I reassured her. "I do, but that's a lot of money."

She laughed. "Not at all! But in that case, how much would you like to tutor my son?"

I played with the cuff on my left hand. I didn't want to ask for money. I had enough pride left to never ask.

She laughed again at my reluctance. "Great, so ten dollars an hour then? Here is our address." She plucked a piece of paper from her purse along with a pen and scribbled something down. She shoved it in my hand as she stood. "I'll be right back Ryder, I need to go to the restroom."

Before I could protest or hand back the paper, she was gone. I sighed and tucked the slip into the vest pocket.

Suddenly I was standing face to face with Ryder. He wore an unpleasant expression. "What the hell?" He growled, pronouncing each word with emphasis and clarity.

"Excuse me?" I asked.

"What the fuck do you think you're doing?" I winced again as he swore and stepped back quickly. He noticed and smirked. "What? Don't like bad words?" He mocked in a child's voice.

I glanced back at the door, hoping his mother would be back soon. "Your mother asked me to tutor you, don't blame me."

"You agreed." He sneered.

I was annoyed, why was he blaming me for needing the money? "Well, it's your fault in the first place for being dumb. Only an idiot would blame someone else for his lack of common sense, but I guess being an idiot yourself, you wouldn't know what common sense is."

He raised an eyebrow in surprise and crossed his arms. "Where's your boss? I wonder what she would say when she finds the host insulting the customer." That's when I remembered where we were and my place. He was the customer and I was his host. I caught my tongue and glowered. But I was scared. Was he going to tell Mrs. Clair?

He must have sensed my predicament and smirked. He looked like he was about to say something but stopped and frowned. Instead, he asked, "Have I met you before?" But he shook his head and spat, "Stay away." before sitting back down in a huff. I backed away and waited against the wall as his mother came back in the room. The host waited on the side in case they needed something as they ate. Now I realized why Kristy complained every time she was the hostess; all you did was stand there. When they were finally done eating, they stood and I opened the door for them.

Mrs. Kenneth placed a hand on my shoulder making me jump. My whole frame tensed. She didn't seem to notice as she commented, "Bye Nathan, your cake is amazing."

Ryder followed close behind. He raised an eyebrow as I visibly relaxed when her touch disappeared, but didn't comment. On his way out he shoved me against the door.

For some reason, the treatment wasn't surprising.

I shook myself off and went straight to cleaning their table. Tomorrow was Monday, and my days had just gotten longer.

Chapter ~Two~

Before I could get to work, or tutoring, I had to survive school. In general, school was a hassle I'd rather avoid. Still, if I didn't do well, I wouldn't be able to get scholarships or get better work later on. The café was only two blocks away, so at least it was a convenient walking distance.

I hung my head down so I looked like any other student and shoved through the packed halls to class. If only it were like the movies, where trouble arrived during class and the teacher could intercept before anything happened.

Instead of making it safely to the room, something pulled me back with a force that sent me sprawling. Kids avoided the scene, knowing too well that this happened often. I looked around carefully, and then decided to get up before I got trampled. I picked myself up but no sooner was I shoved forward. Again, I was on the ground.

Unlike at the café, here, I didn't have to force a smile.

I scrambled to get up and pushed more frantically toward the class. It was in the hall over–in other words, too far.

"Where you running to, Nate?"

Great. I didn't look back but continued forward, trying to make it look like I wasn't running for my life.

I noticed the halls clearing slowly, which also revealed the sound of hurrying steps. I glanced behind and found my pursuers. Sure, they were on the soccer team, but I've been avoiding danger all my life. I swept into class before they could catch me.

Math wasn't a popular subject, so as suspected the few students unlucky enough to be moved to Advanced Algebra resided in the halls until the bell rang and they were forced to enter.

Ms. Richmond glanced up at the abrupt opening of the door. She had brown hair graying at the roots, and metal rim spectacles crowned her hazel eyes. She was by far one of my favorite teachers, and the feeling seemed to be mutual.

"Good morning," I took a needed breath. "Ms. Richmond."

"Good morning Nathan." She put down the papers she was reading and looked at me closely. "Is everything alright?"

I nodded briefly. "Great."

"How's work?"

Again, I found myself wondering, how does everyone know about me? Then I remembered last year. We were given this huge project, involving volunteer work and the percentages from it and whatnot. I couldn't spare the time and reluctantly filled her in on my situation.

"Great." I looked around the room—it was empty. I took a lucky seat on the side.

"Earning enough?"

"Yeah, pay's still good." I thought about something and added, "I'm managing another job now too."

She gave me her full attention. She was like a mother, always understanding and caring. She was much like Mrs. Kenneth, now that I thought about it, but more subdued and quiet.

"Another job? Honestly Nathan, I don't think you can handle it."

I waved her away. "It's just tutoring."

"Who?"

"Some guy named Ryder."

"Ryder Kenneth?" She asked in disbelief.

I raised an eyebrow and nodded. "You know him?"

She chuckled. "Know him? He's my nephew." My jaw dropped. Oh. Oh... "And, he's in this class."

"What?" I was startled. I've never seen him in my class. But if I think about it, I barely knew anybody in my class in the first place. People who weren't in any school sports were usually ignored, so it wasn't like I had any friends in any of my classes.

"He sits in the back." She shook her head. "You've never noticed him?"

"No." I sighed. So I spent half the year not noticing such a jerk? "Wait, you said he's your nephew?"

"Yes, his mother is my sister. How did you manage to become his tutor? He needs it, but I never thought you would volunteer."

"I didn't." I grumbled. "Mrs. Kenneth asked when they came to the café for dessert, and I couldn't refuse."

She laughed. "Very typical. My sister is very persuasive. And always meddling." She adds with an undertone of warning. I didn't understand.

I pulled out yesterday's homework and began today's lesson as the class slowly filled in. I tried to ignore the students as usual, but wanted to be sure whether that idiot was in my class. Why would he take an advanced class if he couldn't handle it?

As I thought this, the dirty blond came walking in and headed for his seat in the back just as his aunt had said.

He must have never noticed me before either. He was smiling like a turd and punching his friends playfully. That's when I noticed, his friends...

I didn't know they were in this class too! If I'd known most of the soccer team was in an advanced class with me, I would have dropped out, or worked harder to get to a higher class they wouldn't be in. Especially if the very people here were the ones who liked to make my life miserable at school.

I slumped lower in the chair. Whenever I came to math, I always thought I'd have escaped the trouble. Well, that didn't work when they were in this class too!

This also got me thinking. Did that mean Ryder was on the soccer team? Then why has he never been with the group as they beat me up? Maybe he had, and I just never noticed.

By the end of class I figured it was best to stay away completely. It seems I'm already on his list, and being at school surrounded by friends that are willing to beat me up, doesn't seem like the best possible situation.

I waited for the class to empty and him to leave. My mind was filled with the goal of not being seen. Which is why by the end of the day, I almost forgot about the sure-to-be nightmare.

After school, I had ten minutes before my shift at the Rose started. Normally, I have to run. I was ready to take off out of the door if I hadn't slammed into something big, and hard, and really familiar.

I'm so dead. I could feel the ache of bruises that haven't faded yet.

The force had sent me sprawling back onto the floor. Marcus can be pretty lazy, so he didn't bother to pick me up for a punch. He just kicked me.

The halls were sadly empty. This only encouraged the soccer players' act of violence.

"Hey fag, where've you been?" I was doubled over and holding my stomach when he decided to put in the effort to haul me up and punch me across the face. Just his voice and language choice had me cowering like an idiot.

I wondered briefly where his friend, Jonah, was, but decided to focus on not getting punched. I wasn't sure why they chose me to bully, but it seemed to bring them obvious joy.

There was a pause in his punch before he decided. "You know what? I'm busy today. No point if Jonah's not here."

He threw me down and I landed hard on my side. Great. It looks like I was going to die tomorrow instead of today.

I got up and ignored the throbbing of my side and checked the time. He made me late. I took off at a sprint down the neighborhood. The limp in my stride wasn't too noticeable, so if I ignored it, surely everyone else would too.

I arrived at the café out of breath but ready to begin work. Kristy met me in the back as I entered.

"Hey Na..." Her smile turned upside down and she strode over to where I stood. "What happened? You're bleeding."

I am? She took a tissue and wiped the corner of my mouth, showing me the blood.

"Oh sorry. I didn't notice when...I fell?" I finished lamely.

She rolled her eyes. "What happened?"

"I fell." I answered more confidently.

"I seriously doubt that unless the ground became alive and punched you. There's a bruise..." She touched the side of my face but I jumped and pulled away. "Who hit you?"

I shrugged. Kristy knew to a degree I got bullied. Despite being the same age, she was very empathetic.

"I'm fine." I went to my locker to retrieve my uniform then before entering the bathroom called, "Get to work."

I closed the door before she could answer and hastily started to change my clothes. I spared a glance in the mirror and stopped, as usual, as I saw the marks on my body. Most of the scars weren't new—some being the long streaks on my back that hadn't faded since a time in my life that I will never really forget. A new bruise was bluing on my stomach. I hurried to pull on my shirt and vest, stopping only momentarily to look at my left wrist.

Some scars don't fade.

Chapter ~Three~

My shift never really ends when it's supposed to. I'd always stay longer for the extra hours, sometimes not leaving until after the café closes. Often, I'd still be cleaning even after Kristy and her grandmother leave.

But today was different and I was slipping on my usual long sleeved shirt earlier than usual. I got my bags and took off out of the café, determined not to be late for tutoring.

The address Mrs. Kenneth gave me showed that they lived in an expensive part of town. I was panting hard when I came to their street.

Not a lot of houses dotted the sides, considering most were huge and had a gate as well as trees blocking my view. I counted the houses until I came to the last one in a cul-de-sac which lost cars probably used to turn around. They had a gate as well, but it stood slightly ajar so I let myself in.

It was big. Maybe ten– no, fifty times the size of my house, which was a simple flat. The white paint blinded me. I knocked, honestly quite nervous, on the double doors.

Mrs. Kenneth answered. She was wearing one of the many sun dresses I've seen her in at the shop and she ushered me in.

"I'm so glad you found our house, it gets quite confusing down this side of the neighborhood." She led me up the stairs to the second floor and down a hallway. She stopped in front of an ordinary door and whispered, "Thank you so much for agreeing to tutor him. Don't let his attitude bother you, he's actually really glad."

I seriously doubted that but didn't voice it. She pushed open the door and peeked inside for Ryder. He must have been in the connecting bathroom because the door was closed and the shower was running. She shepherded me in and smiled before closing the door, marking her leave.

His room was huge, and by huge I mean about the size of my kitchen and room combined. I sat on the bed and for a moment resisted the urge to press my hands against it as deep as possible. It was one of those mattresses that felt like feathers were stuffed inside, and I was slightly insulted that it barely sunk under my weight. I wasn't that scrawny, was I?

I took my books out and a pencil, deciding to get some of my own home-work done before he came out.

It didn't take long. I was on my second page of math when the door opened and he came out in only sweatpants. His hair was dripping and he shook it before he noticed he wasn't the only one in the room.

"What the fuck?" He shouted as he stumbled to his dresser and rummaged for something.

I felt like laughing, but knew better. I covered my mouth that betrayed a small smile. I think he was exaggerating.

He threw the towel that was slung over his shoulder at my face. I fell back on the bed a little dumbstruck. Gross.

"What was that for..." I pushed myself up and picked the towel off my face. He stood in front of me with a glare and his arms crossed over a clean shirt.

"What the hell are you doing here?" He growled.

"Um, tutoring?" I hinted. He frowned before understanding lit his face.

"Oh...yeah." He glowered and went to the corner and slammed down in a beanbag. He was seated in front of a large TV and he pulled out a game controller. He hooked up one of those digital soccer games I've never played or tried to understand.

I cleared my throat to get his attention. He ignored me and pressed start. Music erupted from the attached stereo and he turned it down a notch.

"Hey." I called. Again he ignored me and continued playing.

I was getting annoyed. I was so glad I wasn't obliged to smile and be polite, because I really didn't feel like paying him any respect. Who did this guy think he was? I pushed myself off from the bed with my textbook and paper with answers in either hand. I blocked his vision of the huge TV.

"Do your homework." I commanded.

He scoffed and motioned with the controller. "Get out of my way. My mom will pay; you don't really have to do anything. You're only here for the money right?"

I frowned. I had enough pride to always work for what could be earned. I looked around the room to find his bag on the side of the TV stand. I retrieved it and threw it in his lap.

His temper rose instantly and he glared. "What the hell?"

I pressed the button, turned off the TV, and sat in front of him. "I'm being paid to help you bring your grades up. So your grades will go up. If you try."

He shouted, "Ugh!" and tossed his controller back on the TV stand. I tried to take a discrete deep breath. I'm doing pretty good. He savagely took out his textbook and a paper to write the answers and figure out the problems.

I was surprised he was obliging, but waited for him to answer the first math problem. After a moment of staring at the textbook, he slammed it shut and rubbed his face with both hands.

"I hate this."

"The feelings mutual." I muttered. He glared and I composed myself. I should not get used to talking back. Just because he's rude doesn't mean I have to be, so I moved next to him and used my textbook.

"Okay, first problem. We're using the binomial theorem—"

"Wait, why do you have the same book as me?" He asked, frowning. "This is advanced algebra."

Oh...I forgot.

"I'm...ah, in your class." I finished awkwardly.

"No you're—"

"Come on focus." I pointed at the work again and he sighed.

He wasn't really dumb. He understood for the most part. He just didn't like doing the work, and after the first page of problems, he completely abandoned it and sat back in his beanbag.

"Come on, we're almost done."

"Fuck off." I winced again and moved away. Maybe it's better if I just let him be for a bit after all.

But he obviously noticed and didn't miss a beat. He raised an eyebrow and smirked, "Aw, so you really don't like bad words?" He asked like he had at the café. I didn't answer and took to finishing my own homework. "Hey, answer."

He didn't need an answer. Instead I said, "Answer your own problems, you have two pages left."

I heard him scoff and I made sure to avoid eye contact. Aaah why did I respond? I think he was mad from being forced to study. I felt his eyes on me and tried to ignore it. All of a sudden he asked, "Hey, why's there a bruise on your face?"

His hand appeared in my vision and brushed the bruise and I jumped back, knocking the textbook off the table.

He raised both eyebrows and asked, "Phobia of being touched too?" He laughed, "Pathetic."

"Shut up." I stammered and reached for my textbook. "I'm not the pathetic one here."

He glared and grabbed the front of my shirt. I gasped and clawed at his hands. Maybe I really was that pathetic. I shut my eyes trying to close off his presence.

Nothing came. I peeked my eyes open to find him staring at me. "What's wrong with you?" He asked with crease lines on his forehead.

I pried his fingers off my shirt and sighed in relief when there was space between us.

"You keep flinching." He said annoyed. I don't know why. "Are you mentally off?"

I should leave. I scrambled up and gathered my books in my bag.

"You shouldn't be talking. You can't even finish those simple equations."

That wiped what concern was on his face away. "Calling me dumb?" He snapped.

For a moment, I myself acted very stupid as I walked to the door. But in my defense my heart was pounding and I was trying to drive the topic away from myself. "Yes actually. Dumb, stupid...pathetic, maybe?"

He looked shocked but recovered quickly. I was ready to dart out of the room but he slammed the door I had opened shut. I tried to open it, but with his hand holding it closed, the attempt was useless.

"Let me out." I said turning back to him. I checked my watch. It had been an hour. I was supposed to stay for two.

His temper was explicit now as he glowered. I hadn't noticed before, and now was an odd time to notice, but he was at least a head taller. "You're an idiot." He spat and raised a fist. How grand, I'm going to get punched for the second time today.

With wide eyes I slipped under his arm so I was scrambling to the opposite side of the room.

My arm was yanked back and suddenly my feet weren't touching the ground. Instead I was sinking into the warm mattress and it only sunk this time because he was on top, shoving me with one arm into the sheets. I realized I must've dropped my bag so I couldn't use that to hit him. I couldn't make him budge despite using all my strength. He seemed to notice at the same time and smirked.

"Who's pathetic now?"

Me.

I punched at his chest to get him off but seriously, what could I do? He was huge, compared to my lanky frame he had muscle. Something I knew I would never have. He himself was growing annoyed and grabbed both my hands with one of his own and held them down. I squirmed uncontrollably, but that was just to hide the shivering that began to rip through my body in small waves. His other hand grabbed my hair, to still my body like he wanted me to face him, but that was impossible.

I gave up struggling and laid panting, hoping the punch that would come would be aimed to my stomach. Yeah, I gave up. I'm good at that.

In the moment waiting for the punch, his weight and the hand in my hair reminded me of something, of a time before, when I was younger. A nauseousness crept up my throat that I could not swallow, and slowly the trembles spread through my muscles, which cringed with anxiety. I looked at him with wide eyes. It wasn't Ryder that I saw.

But after a minute passed and a punch didn't come, his face became clear again. I was just confused. This was Ryder, some idiot that couldn't math properly, not anyone else. His anger also slowly dissolved. Soon he was just staring at me in confusion and slight annoyance.

He was frowning deeply now. "Why are you shaking?" Then his eyes narrowed and he muttered, almost to himself, "I have seen you before..."

"Get," I took a deep breath and tried to shove him off, but nothing could be done when my arms were forced above my head. "Off."

He looked confused for a moment as though he forgot his position. Understanding and maybe embarrassment crossed his features and he hurriedly got off and stood at the edge of the bed. I scooted back completely so I was against the headboard, and rubbed my wrists.

Honestly, I can't believe he held my wrist and didn't notice anything.

I tugged on my sleeves warily. He didn't notice anything, right?

"Sorry, I..." He stopped and scratched his brown-blond hair. He looked dumbfounded. He wasn't sure what he was apologizing for, especially when he had been mad about a moment ago. He made a frustrated noise and I held my arms close to myself, as if shrinking into the pillows would make me disappear. He looked entirely confused and reached out.

"What's—"

"Don't hurt me! I yelled while shying away. Because again, for a moment, it wasn't Ryder. All I saw was a hand reaching toward me. Like in those memories, like in those nightmares.

"I'm not going to hurt you." He said in disbelief.

I almost laughed. Did he say he wasn't going to hurt me? Of course he was going to hurt me! He was about to punch me five seconds ago!

"Why are you..." He trailed off. He licked his lips and started again. "Why are you so...scared?" He finished with an uncertain voice.

"Why wouldn't I– I mean...I'm not scared. " I lied and pulled on my stretched out sleeves one last time. "You were...I'm just...I don't like being touched."

"Or cuss words apparently." He scoffed but stopped when he saw I wasn't sharing his amusement. "Sorry. I'm sorry I scared you."

I looked at him in the eye and tried to gauge if he was sincere. It didn't matter. I muttered, "I said I wasn't."

"Then what then?" He asked curiously as he sat down. The bed sunk under his weight, like the mattress was mocking me.

"Why do you care? You tried to punch me just now."

He shook his head hurriedly. "I didn't mean it, it was instinct because you were annoying. I've been told I have a slight temper–" he seemed to think about it for a second then added, "although I don't really think I do. That's just how I am with my friends." He admitted and sighed, running a hand through his hair. "Actually, it wasn't even you, I was just angry."

"No kidding. That's how jocks interact? God, that's so–"

But before I finished my insult, I suddenly remembered where I was and my purpose in being here. Sure, I didn't have to pretend to be polite. But until now all I've done was upset him. This is a job, Nathan! I was supposed to be tutoring, not insulting him. Would Mrs. Kenneth fire me? Of course she would, on the spot. What if she stopped coming to the café? I would be the reason for losing a regular! "Nevermind. I'm...sorry, too. I didn't mean anything. Don't tell Mrs. Kenneth, please."

He looked at me weirdly.

"Tell mom what, that I got most of my homework done? And here I was looking forward to seeing her face."

There was a moment of silence. Then a nervous laugh escaped. It was a way to relieve the tension. He smiled but was looking at me strangely.

"What?"

He shook his head. "Nothing." He got up and walked over to the beanbag and looked at his homework. "I guess I'll finish."

"Really?" I asked in disbelief. He didn't look back but I could see his smirk in the reflection of the TV. He seemed different all of a sudden, somehow.

Maybe it was because I didn't expect him to apologize. Maybe he was just slow to process his emotions. I don't know what he was thinking, but he seemed less like a...jerk.

What just happened?

Chapter ~Four~

I waited for class to begin. I was exhausted. I stayed up late cleaning the house, and then woke up early just to get to school before Marcus and Jonah. I've done this for the past two days. Ms. Richmond seemed surprised to see me this early again and asked if I was getting enough sleep, pointing out the circles under my eyes were deeper than usual this morning.

I collapsed at my desk and rested my head on my arms. I was tired, but hopefully by the end of the day I'd have enough motivation to go to work. I groaned. Then I have to go tutor the idiot, then go home and clean the mess I made this morning when rushing to school.

After endless minutes of waiting, the bell finally rang and the students reluctantly filed in. I noticed Ryder come in with the two other soccer players I know quite well.

He scanned the seats and when he found me, stopped walking. I raised an eyebrow as if saying– see? I wasn't lying. He didn't make any acknowledgement and kept an indifferent face and continued walking toward his own desk with his friends.

Markus nudged Jonah and they looked in my direction. Their expression told me to look out.

So I did. I ran out of class before anyone else had even packed their back and ran to science, praying for no hassle. I glanced behind once, but they weren't there. I was probably safe.

I'm seriously kidding myself.

A hand shot out from the janitor's closet and my vision went dark. Two people, I sensed, ambushed me, and it was pretty obvious who those two were.

One of the fists found my stomach in the dark. It was amazing they could still aim just fine without vision. Something slammed into my face and I fell back with a crash against the wall. They settled on kicking. At first it hurt but soon I was too numb to notice. But I did notice when the wooden broom struck my back and jabbed at my ribs.

When the seemingly endless beating ceased I opened my eyes. Two shadowy figures could be made out in the dark room.

"Take that Strauss." I heard Jonah spat. The door opened and their figures retreated into the light.

The air slowly entered my lungs again and I became aware of the throbbing pain. I couldn't move, even if I dared. So I just lay there in the dark. I wiggled my fingers and my toes, but just propping myself up sent me coughing and I fell back against the wall. Ah, what was the point? I was late for class. They were probably going over homework. Did I finish the homework? It's so dark in here. Only a sliver of light carried through from under the door.

I gasped. The bell was ringing. Did I fall asleep? Probably, because in sleep, you can't really feel the pain.

I used the wall as a guide to get up and found the door. My ribs were screeching, not as loud as my right hand. I opened the door and instantly received a headache from the sudden light. I forced myself to walk through the hallway at a brisk pace. My limp was worse than the day before.

I checked my watch. That was the after school bell, and I was late for work–really late. Thirty minutes?

I felt something burn in the middle of my throat. I knew the feeling, like you could start sobbing at any moment. I took a deep breath and squinted my eyes shut because, as usual, there's no time. I couldn't run but did my best to quickly walk the blocks to the café.

I avoided Kristy and went through the back. I shut the bathroom door behind me and looked at my reflection. There was a nasty scratch on my cheek. I hope it wouldn't affect my host image. I cleaned away the blood and took off my shirt. Ew. Ew ew. Bruises were added to my already scared back and torso. I pulled on the uniform and again felt the throbbing in my fingers. Maybe if I just stretch them out...NO, no, that was a bad idea.

I went out to the front and walked as inconspicuously as possible. Kristy was making a beeline for me.

"Where have you been?" She asked.

"Sorry, I got distracted at school."

But she didn't look mad. She looked angry.

"Why is your face scratched?" She asked. She looked me in the eyes. "Nathan, did you get in a fight? With who?"

It's not really a fight when I stood no chance. "I'm fine. Sorry I'm late. What tables do you want me to take?"

"If you're not feeling well, I can take–"

"Kristy," I showed my fake smile I was so good at and laughed. "Are you trying to take my customers? Come on. Looks like it's getting busy."

She looked at me doubtfully and slightly offended. "Take the booths."

I nodded and walked off, but she called quietly, "You're even limping!"

I ignored her and walked up to the booth. "Good evening, my names Nathan and I'll be your host for today. What would you be having today?" My smile played on my lips as I kept my head down and focused on my notepad. I didn't want any of the customers to notice the scratch.

"Who knew Strauss worked at a fag café." My head snapped up.

Every muscle in my body told me to run to the back, and I even took a step back before composing myself again. Three people occupied the booth, three soccer players I was familiar with for a variety of reasons.

One of which I was tutoring after work, and the other two the very people who knocked me unconscious this morning.

"Makes sense, considering he's a fag himself." I flinched at Jonah's comment. I wasn't quite sure what a 'fag' was, but I know it could mean to work hard, which I do work hard. Or it could mean cigarette, which didn't make any sense. Recently I found out it could mean a bundle of wood, but why would you call someone a bundle of wood?

The two boys were smirking. I glanced at Ryder. He just stared at me. He was the least nauseous to look at, so his annoyingly blank stare helped me force the smile back on my face so I could keep up the act. "Have you decided what you'd like?"

"Look at that. He actually cleans up quite nicely after what he went through."

"Considering what he went through, I doubted he'd be able to walk properly. Spin for us Strauss, I thought I saw a limp."

I bit my lip, taking a deep breath.

"Doesn't look like he can speak either. Some host. Yeah, good fag should stay silent. He's more of a...maid." Jonah laughed. "That's how he's talking to us right now, like he's our maid. Isn't that right, Ms. Strauss?"

What was I doing? I was just standing there with my head hung, clutching the notepad like it would defend me. Sure, I was embarrassed these two nutjobs found out I worked at a café, considering students shouldn't even be working. Surely they would hold this against me in the future. I was also mad because I couldn't do anything. I was supposed to smile and treat these absolute jerks like guests.

"What would you like?" I repeated with that fake, forced smile and willed my eyes to stay dry. I can hold it in. I can hold in this much.

"Looks like that's all he can say." Jonah taunted. "Look at him, all he can do is smile. Markus, I think we should do something about that–"

"I'd like a pasta and coke." Ryder interrupted indifferently as he looked at the menu. Markus and Jonah looked at him as though waiting for him to add something. He seemed to notice when he looked up. "What, you want me to say 'please, fag?' Come off it." Of course, I flinched. But I kept myself composed. It wasn't so bad since it wasn't fully directed at me.

The other two ordered, and Jonah added a, "Make it quick, Ms. Strauss."

I swallowed my pride and walked off to the kitchen. I knew they were watching, and smirking at my limp.

I returned with their hot food and drinks. They mostly ignored me as they ate fast and I worked the surrounding booths. I swear they didn't even wait for the food to cool. They seemed to have finished eating and were only talking. I reluctantly went over to clear their table.

They were talking about soccer as I stacked their plates with leftover food and half filled cups on a tray. I ignored Jonahs comment, "See, he'd make a good maid." And balanced the tray carefully in my two hands.

I turned to walk back to the kitchen but my foot caught on something and suddenly I was sent crashing to the floor. There was a thunderous collision of dishes on tile.

I gasped and looked around at the mess. The food and drinks had spilled all over my clothes and floor. Almost all the dishes and glass had shattered. I looked up at Jonah who was close to rolling out of the booth, laughing.

Everyone was staring. Kristy came running over but stopped a few feet away because of the dangerous shards of glass.

"Nathan, what happened?" She asked. Then she gasped and covered her mouth with her hands. "My god, you're hands..."

"I– I'm s–sorry." I ignored the stares and scrambled to my knees and began hazardously gathering the multitude of shards. My hands were shaking violently.

"Stop Nathan, you're bleeding!"

"I'm sorry. I tripped. Sorry." I repeated up at her and the surrounding cus-tomers. I gathered most of the glass onto the tray and completely ignored my ruined uniform. I was too embarrassed to look up at a satisfied Jonah. What had I ever done to him?

I picked up the tray and rushed to get to the kitchen. Kristy followed me into the back.

I threw away the broken dishes and took the plates that hadn't shattered to the sink. Kristy stopped me and forced me to slow down and breathe. I was freaking out.

"Nathan, calm down. Let me look at your hands." She urged.

"Its fine."

"Will you stop saying that?" She almost shouted. "Look, you're bleeding!" She dragged it under the running water and I winced. I just noticed how badly I had hurt my hands. They were scrapped from the ground and cut up, spilling blood where the glass cut my skin. The kitchen door swung open and an elderly woman burst in.

Mrs. Clair wasn't as old as people make her sound. Her face consisted of many lines, but that was natural. She shared the same blond hair as her granddaughter but the top was graying. I couldn't read her green eyes.

"Mrs. Clair, I'm so sorry. I didn't mean to drop the dishes, I tripped and it just..." I trailed off. She stopped next to me with her hands on her hips, and I prepared for a scolding. I was freaking out because I was afraid of being fired. I cannot be fired.

Instead, she took my hands and examined it carefully.

"Are you okay?" She asked.

She took a tweezers and looked skeptically at my hand. She pinched the skin and out came a tiny, shiny piece of glass. I was thankful she held my wrist with my sleeves drawn over.

"I'm sorry about the broken dishes. I'll pay for it—"

"Don't be ridiculous Nathan. As long as you're okay, it's fine." She shook her head and examined my hands once again. "Though you aren't one to trip...what happened to your face?"

"It's just a scratch." I muttered.

She raised an eyebrow at me disbelievingly but dropped the subject. She moved my hands under the water to wash off the remaining blood.

"The bandages are in the back room—"

"It's okay. It doesn't hurt." Badly. I caught sight of the wall clock and widened my eyes. "Shoot, I'm late. Mrs. Clair, I forgot to mention I have another job, so I wont be able to stay late during the week."

She smiled kindly. "Julia told me you were tutoring her son. It's fine, but make sure you still have a life after all these jobs."

Adults worry too much. Kristy followed me to the back room and was rummaging for the first aid kit.

"That guy tripped you, didn't he?"

"What guy?" I muttered as I retrieved my clothes.

"In the booth. He was laughing at you." She seethed. "Is he the one beating you up?"

"No one's beating me up, Kris. I got to hurry, I'm late for tutoring."

She backed off a little, and then jumped up again. "Wait, Grandma said you were tutoring Mrs. Kenneth's son. Wasn't that him at the table?" She narrowed her eyes. "If he plans any—"

I laughed. "I think you're over exaggerating." Although, who really knows?

She stopped and mulled it over. "Yeah probably. Only that one asshole was laughing. The other two did not look happy. But if you need back up in a fight," She crossed her arms readily, "You have me."

I gave a small laugh. What a great friend. Kristy went to a private school across town, so it wasn't like she saw me other than at work. Despite that, she's been looking over me ever since she found out about my situation.

Part of my situation. I hated my situation.

I pushed those thoughts out of mind and changed before Kristy could find the first aid kit and hold me back, then took off out of the café. The throbbing in my leg reminded me it wasn't smart to run in this condition.

It's not so bad, I thought. I was just a little tired. Just...a little bit. I just had to get through two hours of tutoring.

An idiot, I reminded myself. Just what I needed.

The size of their house stole my breath just as it had the day before. I would never have imagined myself stepping foot in a house like this. I knocked on the door and it was about three minutes before there was a response.

Instead of Mrs. Kenneth, a boy maybe one year older than me opened the door. He raised his eyebrows.

"Yeah?"

I opened and closed my mouth. "I'm...Ryder's tutor?"

He nodded slowly as he looked me up and down, assessing me. "Okay, come in." He held the door open wider.

"Are you Ryder's brother?" I asked, though I doubted it. He had black hair and dark eyes, and dressed nicer than someone would at home.

"Hell no." He laughed. "I'm Mattson, their steward." He paused and corrected, "Or butler I guess. Kind of. Mrs. Kenneth offered me the job when I applied to her company as a janitor."

"Oh." I said and thought briefly to earlier when Jonah called me a maid. Butler is a better term. The Kenneth's were really wealthy. "Nice to meet you."

"The pleasures mine." He smiled easily in a way that made his eyes wink. "Do you know the way to Mr. Doosh's room?"

I bit my lip. Wow, some butler, calling his employer a doosh. "Yeah, I can find my way." He nodded and left me to trace my steps from yesterday up to the second floor and down the hall. I knocked this time.

"Who's it?" An annoyed voice called.

"Your tutor." There was some noise on the other side before he called, "Well don't just stand there."

I opened the door slowly, afraid he might annoyed already. But he was just sitting in the beanbag. It looked like he was playing his video games, and only now took out a blank sheet of paper for homework. At least he was willing to work today.

I didn't say anything but went to sit on his bed. It's not like I sensed any immediate danger, but I already got beat up once today and wasn't too sure if my bad luck had run out yet. It was somehow too much pressure to be near him, even if he hadn't really done anything. Just knowing he saw my moment of weakness earlier in front of his friends was rather embarrassing.

I took out my books and a paper. "Question one, x–"

"Why are you sitting over there?" He asked.

"Why not?"

He frowned at my answer and got up, falling on the opposite end of the bed.

"I can't solve it on my own, you can't help from far away."

"Whatever." I muttered. I looked back at the paper and began solving problems to explain after. For a while we did math, then I helped him with English and Science. Apparently, math wasn't the only class we shared, though we were in different periods. I felt his eyes on me but ignored it. I said as little as possible and kept my voice monotone the entire lesson. Today was rough, so I'm sure he can imagine why I wasn't being very polite or smiley. For some reason my mind kept wondering back to the cafe and the moment when he said that one word. How did he say it again? Did he actually call me that, or was he addressing his friends?

"Are your hands okay?" He asked suddenly.

I shrugged.

"It looks like it hurts to write."

I shrugged again. It hurts because this morning I was beat up by your friends in a janitors closet. Then it had a pretty good glass shower this afternoon because of the said friends.

"Why didn't you get it bandaged? Don't you dare shrug."

So demanding. I didn't shrug. I didn't answer either. He should be focusing on work.

"Jeez, I'm trying to make a conversation but it doesn't work when you don't respond."

I looked him in the eye and answered indifferently, though I was powerless when I flinched just forcing the word out. "I've been told 'fags' should stay silent"

He looked shocked and maybe hurt. He glared and took my writing hand, forcing the pencil to fall. He looked at the cuts carefully. I was about to pull away when he noticed, "It's swollen."

"No it's not."

"Yes..." Then unexpectedly he grabbed my other hand to compare the two.

Only after a moment did I realize he was touching my bare hands with his own. I shot down that brief moment after remembering that this is dangerous. I yanked backward, but he just grabbed on tighter. My frantic tugging only made my long sleeves fall back. Now I was still, praying he wouldn't notice the one thing I wanted to avoid.

But of course, nothing ever works out in my favor. And despite how dumb he was, he had eyes. While looking back and forth between the two, his eyes traveled beyond my palms' and rested on my left hand, or, wrist, to be exact.

"What the hell is that?" He almost shouted and during his distraction, I pulled my hands away with a force that almost sent me falling off the bed.

"Nothing." I cowered and pulled down my sleeves.

He saw, oh god he saw. No one has ever seen.

"Why are there scars–?"

Chapter ~Five~

" **A** re you suicidal?" He asked. "You try to kill yourself?"

What kind of insensitive...

"I've never tried to kill myself." I said indignantly. Then added, "you're seeing things."

I check the clock. Two hours had already passed, but I hadn't stopped the session since he was actually focused. I got up and grabbed my bag.

"Wait, don't you dare leave yet." He scrambled off the bed and blocked my way to the door. "Why did you slit your wrists?"

"I didn't slit my wrist." I clutched my bag tightly because my hands were trembling. "Now may I leave?"

"No." Then he reached for me but I jumped back. He frowned and demanded, "Let me see your wrist."

"No." He lunged for me but I ran backward to get to the other side of the room. "No!"

"Hold still!" For a soccer player, he wasn't that quick. When he moved away from the door I maneuvered around him and was almost able to reach the doorknob when something grabbed my waist from behind. I kicked and thrashed but it was in vain. He held me to the spot and grabbed my wrist, holding it out above my head so he could have a good look.

"You did cut yourself." He breathed. Then suddenly he yelled, "Why the fuck did you cut yourself?"

I flinched and cowered from the harshness of his voice and how close he was.

"I keep telling you, I didn't cut myself." I shouted.

"Then do you mind explaining what the hell is with the fucking scars across your veins?"

"I don't have to explain anything to you." His grip on my wrist tightened and I gasped.

"Explain."

"Why?" I tried to free my other arm from his hold around my waist. Why was I so weak?

"Because I want to know." His voice went quiet all of a sudden.

"No." I glared at nothing. "You're going to use it against me." Because that's just how the world works, someone discovers your secrets and suddenly you're powerless.

"I promise I won't. I'm not like that." The grip loosened and I was spun around, face-to-face with him. I backed up and bumped into the bed, sitting down harshly.

"To others. What about fags?" I flinched again at the word. He glared. What exactly did it mean? All I know is that it was derogatory in some way and it meant I'd get punched a second later.

"Don't say it if you're scared of it." He muttered. "Now are you going to tell me or not?"

"Not."

He laid a hand on either side of me and leaned close. "Listen, I don't have any intention of weaponizing your secret, and I'm not going to leave it because...because I don't feel like it. So just tell me why you tried to fucking kill yourself or what I can do to make you stop."

"First of all, I didn't try to kill myself. And second," I breathed and looked down, before continuing a little more quietly, "Do you mind not swearing? Geez...and back up a little."

I played with my long sleeve and tugged it over my hands. I looked up at his bright gray eyes that assessed me, a little too long if you asked me.

"Talk. What's the reason? Is there a reason?"

"If I give you a reason, will you stop annoying me?"

"I'd probably still annoy you, but I'll stop asking about it."

I nodded slowly and sighed, breathing deeply. "Fine. The reason there are scars on my wrist, is because...at a time, it had been cut."

There was silence as he mulled over my words, then suddenly, "No fucking duh!"

I flinched and he stopped his brief rampage, straightened, and paced the room. "Did you cut yourself?"

"I gave you a reason, I am not obliged to answer any more questions." Not that I needed to in the first place, but I knew that would annoy him and hopefully be the end to the interrogation.

"Fine." He jabbed. "Then tell me why you're scared of swearing."

"No more questions." I muttered.

"No, I said no more questions about 'it', implying your wrist. I'm asking about another one of your phobias."

"I don't have any phobias!".

He stared me straight in the eye and spat, "Fuck."

I winced.

"Could've fooled me."

I looked at him closely. A part of me was obviously starting to get used to his weird behavior, but I still had no reason to share anything. It would only make me worse off. "I can't tell you."

He must have noticed a change in my voice because he eyed me carefully.

"Too personal or because you don't trust me?"

Both. "Too personal." Then I muttered. "Way too personal."

"Then can I ask what my friends meant when they said, 'after what he went through' at the cafe?"

Again, I don't see why he would care. It was Jonah doing everything, but he went along as well. One day, I'm going to look up after a beat down and he's going to be there laughing with the rest of them.

"I have to go." I whispered.

"Where?"

"Um, home?"

I could think of a million reasons I could use if he asks 'for what?' I still have to clean. Maybe I can make some food for the next day so I have an actual meal. But he didn't ask anything else, so I got up, slung my bag over my shoulder and walked out, feeling his eyes trained on me the entire time.

—

—

I managed to evade running into Jonah and Marcus at school. I try not to run though. It makes it too obvious where I am and that I'm avoiding them. Plus, lately running hasn't been doing my body any good. It could be because of lack of sleep, but even the smallest stresses were making me dizzy.

Ryder hasn't asked much more questions. He does stare at me like I'm about to kill myself though. Kristy keeps a close eye on me as well. It makes me wonder when I've started worrying about all these things, and when all these people have begun worrying about me. Before, all that mattered was making the money needed to get by.

It still is.

Though I don't know why. Sometimes things get too hard, and even making enough money wears me out completely till the point I need to skip school for a couple of days. It makes me ask myself whether it was worth being saved by the doctors.

Yeah, it would have been nice to just die then. But I didn't, so here I am, working like my life depended on it.

Living alone was only one of the reasons why I needed to earn money. The other reason was...not as easy to deal with.

I had a rough cough by the time I got home. Ryder got frustrated today and it took longer for him to finish homework. I had to practically re-teach the entire chapter. I never get sick but this was probably my unluckiness as usual. I've always been able to handle work and school more or less. Maybe tutoring was maxing my limit.

I closed the door behind me, and as usual it echoed through the flat. It looked as if the house were deserted. I lived alone, completely alone and didn't have any belongings, only essentials. I dropped my bag on the floor and collapsed on the couch. There was a moment of eerie silence before I began coughing again. Hopefully it's just a cold.

"Sounds like someone's coming down with a cold."

I jumped off the couch when the low voice interrupted the should-be silent house. I scrambled to my feet and searched for the owner that had gone unnoticed upon me entering.

My heart raced and my eyes were wide as I backed up slowly when I found him coming out from the kitchen.

"What do you eat? There's absolutely nothing in the fridge." He grumbled with a smile.

He's back. He wasn't supposed to be back for a couple of months, what was he doing here?

"You look scared Nathan, I wonder why." He said thoughtfully.

I didn't respond. I couldn't my tongue felt fat and stuck in my throat. "No welcome back hug?" He asked as he walked forward with outstretched arms.

I jumped back and cowered against the wall. He smirked and stopped a few feet away.

Finally I found my voice and managed to whisper, "Payday isn't until the end of the month."

He hung his head, but his smile stayed where it was. "I got back early and thought you'd be delighted to know. After all, I doubt you'd have enough money to meet pay day."

"I'll be able to pay it." I grimaced, thinking about the extra income from tutoring Ryder. Suddenly I didn't mind his frustration from this evening. It wasn't that bad at all. I should have stayed longer.

"You think?" He asked, taking a step closer. "Last month you couldn't, or the month before. You can barely keep this...apartment, if you can even call it that. If you want, I can always loan some cash where it's needed–"

"I am not borrowing money from you. My father did a grand enough job of that already." I glared and suddenly he was in front of me

In that instant my breath was gone. I sagged, with the help of his fist holding me up. He shoved me against the wall and grabbed my chin so I faced him.

"Now, it's rude to interrupt Nathan. Your dad was a smart man, other than..." He grabbed my wrist with his free hand so he had a clear view of the scars. "Certain decisions."

I yanked my exposed wrist from his grip. He frowned at this. "They're just scars Nathan, nothing to be ashamed of." He smiled evenly but it didn't reach his eyes. "After all, I've seen the others."

Everything blurred momentarily as I was yanked around him and pushed to the couch. In a moment he was on me and pinned my arms above my head. His free hand traced the skin that was left exposed when my shirt snagged up.

"Stop!" I screamed.

"That was the other thing I came to talk to you about. Why not push up the payday? Since you won't be able to pay as usual, why not try that other method of compensation?"

On some level I knew I was shaking. My shirt was lifted further up and he could clearly see the healed scars. He leaned closer as his hand reached behind and lightly circled the old belt marks.

"Please, no...not..." I whimpered uselessly. He leaned down and I jerked my head to the right, but he didn't seem to mind as his lips found my neck. His hand now circled the small of my back and my spine arched in disgust.

Ryder was right. I was pathetic.

"Stop...please..." But his fingers slowly traveled up my spine. My shirt was half on and his lips fluttered on my cheekbone when hysteria forced me to yell, "I'll make the money!" Then whimpered once again, "So please, stop. Not again."

He lifted his face away and I dared a peek. He was smiling doubtfully when he said, "Fine, if you believe you can make the cash. But remember, money isn't the only way to pay." He got up and I curled into myself. "You look adorable when you cry." He wiped the tears away with his gloved thumb. When had I begun crying? "Soon, Nathan. Until then, goodbye."

I shut my eyes and only relaxed slightly when the door slammed shut.

~~~

hy hy :) taking a break, I'll uploading the next few chapters later tonight. Thank you for reading!
~~~

Chapter ~Six~

Mrs. Clair was in the office in the back and I was opening the shop. I decided to do overtime this morning.

The man that had come by last night was Mr. Stevens, and his words shoved me on overdrive. I completely neglected my symptoms, mostly because I didn't have money to buy over-the-counter medicine. Every month I pay him money for rent and a portion of a much bigger debt that, should I think about, would make me faint. My dad had borrowed money off of him for years; resulting in the huge tab.

But my dad is gone.

Now I have to pay back the entire loan, which could take my whole life. Mr. Stevens is powerful in the sense he has back up. He could make me lose everything I barely have a hold on right now. He's not related, or at least I hope not. Apparently he was an old 'friend' of dad. He's very controlling. If I'm not able to make payday by the end of the month, he finds other ways to compensate.

And that's what scares me.

For the first couple of months he gave simple violent reminders and made a mess of the house, since I was young. But then he changed it to a much more personal payment.

I guess Ryder was right to call it a phobia. But he wasn't the only reason I don't like being touched. The other reason was my dad.

When I was nine my mother passed. My dad took the news horribly. He began drinking heavily until he just collapsed. He quit his job and continuously used Mr. Stevens' money to pay for his gambles, drugs, and other payments. He was always wasted, so I had already begun learning life for myself and cooked, cleaned, walked myself to school. Reducing his burden wasn't enough. He took out all his anger on the only person he could find–me.

He would punch, kick, and whip me with his belt until I bled. I believe he was barely aware of what he was doing. Once he had used the rod from the curtains, if I cry he would come back.

I don't know what changed one day, but he finally decided to end it. He came home half dead, with his eyes sunken into the back of his head and a grimace outlining his features. I had made dinner, because at the time I had given up and decided to just go on like nothing happened to me every night. He had given me a long look.

"You look like her," He drawled. "And someone else."

I did look like my mother. But I looked like him as well.

He ambled slowly forward and swiped a knife from the table. I stumbled backward but he grabbed my small arm with a grip so strong I shouted. He shook me and yelled, "You're nobody! You're the reason she's gone!" He raised the knife and sliced down the front of my shirt.

The blade tore into my skin and I screamed. "Why don't you just die?"He asked in a shout. I couldn't move from that spot at his feet. Before he plunged the knife through me, he gave me a last look. I could tell why he hesitated to stab me: because I looked like his wife. So instead he dropped to his knees, raised the knife, and sliced my wrist repeatedly.

I remember lying in my pooling blood. There were lights flashing outside. My dad looked aghast at what he'd done, though I don't know why since he's always wanted to get rid of me. I remember him plunging the knife through his neck before I lost consciousness.

Somehow the doctors were able to stem the blood flow and stitch up the slices done to my wrist. In other words, I lived. The same couldn't be said for my father.

I don't remember anything from the hospital, or until after when I met Mr. Stevens. I wasn't sure about the whole custody thing since I was eleven, but for some reason, since then, I've lived on my own. That man probably had his own hand in it, which I found strange considering I've never really met him before and we weren't related. Mr. Stevens brought the debt up when I was thirteen. And, as anyone could have guessed, that's when I began working for my life.

Mr. Stevens is cruel, and likes to take advantage of my failure in creating the money needed.

Not one of my scars were caused by me. Mr. Stevens won't let me die, I'm scared the doctors will save me once again, and I'll be back in the horrid hospital. Mr. Stevens will probably pay my medical bill and increase the debt. Then the chances of being free will vanish like my hope long ago.

I coughed in my shirt so I wouldnt get germs on the dishes I was preparing. It's useless thinking about the past—something I have no control over. This month I had to make the payday. I will not be taken advantage of again.

"Nathan, why are you coughing so much? I can hear it from my office."
Mrs. Clair came out with her reading glasses propped on her nose and her
hands on her hips. "Are you getting sick?"

"No, I'm fine." I smiled.

She rolled her eyes and felt my forehead before I could evade. "You're
flushed and burning up. Go home right now and get some rest."

"Mrs. Clair, I can't. I need the money."

"I know you do, but I don't want you fainting on the job. Being sick doesn't
help you or anyone else. Go." She pointed toward the door. I groaned and
obliged.

Fine, I thought. I'll go to school then. For once I took my time. My eyes
drooped and suddenly I slammed into something solid. I blinked and
looked up.

Huh, I was at school already. So that's what its like to sleepwalk.

"Watch where you're–oh, hello Nathan." I looked up at the person I had
run into.

It was the boy from the other day. "Hi, Mattson right?" I looked around
and asked, "You come to this school?"

He nodded. "I transferred a couple days ago." I nodded slowly and stifled a
yawn. He looked me up and down. "Are you feeling okay? You don't look
so good."

"Thanks." I mumbled.

He threw an arm around my shoulders unexpectedly and I flinched. He
didn't notice and continued speaking. "Don't get me wrong, I think you
look cute. But you seem under the weather."

I felt under the weather and...wait, did he just say I looked cute? "Did you just–"

"What period do you have first?" He interrupted and began walking toward the building doors.

"Um..." I stumbled for words. His arm was making me panic with alarm. "Uh, English."

He nodded and smiled slyly. "Me too. And I know you're in my math class, don't know why its last today." I tried to shrug off his arm but he ignored the attempt.

"Where's your locker?" I asked.

He pointed down the hall and I sighed with relief as I stepped away. "I'll catch up then, I have to get my books." He nodded slowly before walking away.

What was that about?

I shook my head and found my locker. Before I put some books in my bag I was shoved to the side. My bag fell and a bunch of papers scattered. I looked up to see Jonah and Marcus snickering. Ryder was coming up behind them. He was about to go on as if it was normal for his friends to act like that–which it was–but then he caught my eye.

He stopped behind the two and I wondered briefly what he would do.

Nothing, of course he would do nothing. It doesn't especially bother me. He can say he's worried about me during tutoring, but it shouldn't change how we act in school. Plus, I hadn't been exactly nice to him. I was probably still trash in his eyes.

"Hello, Ms. Strauss." Marcus mocked and I scrambled to collect my papers and avoid their taunts.

"Will you be serving us again this afternoon?" Jason asked with his arms crossed.

"Nah, he probably got fired after he broke those plates. No point in is going." Marcus said half heartedly, pulling out his phone to look at something more interesting.

"I didn't break them, you tripped me." I muttered. Jason rolled his eyes.

"Or, you're too weak to carry an empty plate." He laughed.

"You're weaker if you need someone else to back you up." I murmured quietly. Apparently, their hearing was better than their brains and they heard my comment.

Marcus reached down and grabbed my left wrist to yank me up. My mind seared with clarity as memories returned.

I shouted, "Let go! Stop, let go-" while trying with all my effort to pull away. "Hey-" Ryder began as he stepped forward grabbing Marcus' shoulder. Is this where he joins his friends? I was shoved against the locker and Jonah grabbed a hand full of my shirt.

"Say that again." He raised his fists and for a moment the look in his eyes reminded me of my father.

"St–"

"What's going on?" A voice asked from behind.

I was dropped to the ground and suddenly I could breathe again. The three turned to look at Mattson coming up from our left.

"Mattson?" Ryder asked in confusion.

"Who're you?" Jason asked.

"Hello Mr. Kenneth. Fancy seeing you here." Mattson said indifferently. He smiled but it was obviously fake and his eyes looked venomous.

"Who's he?" Marcus asked.

"Nobody." Ryder sneered.

"Nathan are you okay?" Mattson shoved past the other boys and offered a hand. I picked up my bag and got up by myself.

Jonah scoffed and stalked off with Marcus right behind. Ryder dawdled.

Mattson began brushing me off but I jumped at his touch and suddenly someone else was blocking my vision. Ryder grabbed Mattson's hand.

He muttered something and Mattson smiled not exactly pleasantly, and I was confused.

"What?" I asked. The two looked down at me. Why was everyone taller than me? I was pretty tall myself at 5'6", and yes that's tall in my book.

Ryder didn't say anything but stepped away, glaring at Mattson. The latter stepped closer to me and swung an arm casually over my shoulders. Of course, I gripped my books and put some space between our bodies but he didn't seem to catch it.

Ryder's glare intensified.

I was...confused. Why was Mattson even around me? Was he latching on to the only person he knew?

"I need to get to class." I muttered and hurriedly left Mattson's side to scurry down the hall. Honestly I wasn't quite sure why either of them was acting strange, but I didn't care.

I was too tired and exhausted to care.

Plus, Mr. Stevens was back, and expecting payment—any sort of payment. I shouldn't be distracted with anything else.

Chapter ~Seven~

"**N**athan, are you sleeping?" I heard my name but didn't raise my head. It was too heavy. "Nathan?"

Huh, it sounded like Ms. Richmond.

Wait...my head snapped up. Shoot, I was still in class. "I'm sorry Ms. Richmond. Please continue."

She gave me a worried look as the class snickered at my back. I must have looked exhausted. My chest tickled with the need to cough but I resisted the urge. I rubbed my eyes forced myself to focus on the lesson. Ten more minutes before school was over...

Ten more minutes.

"Remember, if you didn't get it done during class its due tomorrow, first thing. You're dismissed."

Everyone sprang up, including me. My head swam dizzily and I steadied myself with the desk.

I hadn't finished the class work. That meant I either need to get it done at Ryder's, when I still have to do the other homework, or afterward.

"Nathan?" Ms. Richmond called me. I grabbed my bag and walked over to her desk. "What's going on? You should've stayed home if you're sick."

I smiled. "I'm not sick. Don't worry Ms. Richmond; I'm as up as ever. I have to get to work. Bye."

I was out of there before she could mumble a goodbye.

I took off out of the building, time for work.

.~*~. RYDER .~*~. (HAH! DIDN'TEXPECT THAT!)

I looked at my watch. He was late. He was never late, that much I knew.

I thought back to the first time I met him. My mom did that on purpose. She practically dragged me to that stupid café, saying there was someone she wanted me to meet. I thought she meant her friend Mrs. Clair, who I already knew. Not some boy who gave me sudden clarity on the type I found attractive.

I wasn't exactly straight. I was bi, not that anyone knew.

And no way was I letting him know that. His personality doesn't fit him. Who was I to know my mom would suddenly ask him to tutor me? And that he'd be super annoying about it.

I didn't completely mind.

The first time he came by I had totally forgot and came out shirtless. He caught me off guard. I learned he tried not to speak before he thinks but sometimes when I annoy him it escapes.

I couldn't help but touch the cut on his face, and at that contact he jumped back. I was beyond curious as to why he was afraid of swearing and being touched. It was none of my business. He had no reason to fulfill my selfish curiosity.

Especially because I completely ignored him at school. I caught his eye but couldn't go over. He looked at me like I was going to beat him up. Which is valid since I almost punched him for goodness sake, twice, and threatened him. My friends seemed to hate his guts as well.

I hadn't meant to take them to the café. I was complaining about my mom taking me, and they decided to check it out. It was annoying seeing him force that smile as Jason insulted him. Who the fuck did Jason think he was talking to? Was this treatment normal? He was trembling and bleeding, and looked so hopeless.

Then there was today. Had those two been beating him up before? I was a jerk, but I've never really joined one of those incidents. It was just dumb.

I was about to stop the situation, but then Mattson that son of a bitch stepped in. He moved to town with his uncle or something and being the amazing and kind woman my mom was, offered him a job. When did he begin being friends with Nathan?

Nathan was incredibly dense for a boy. Didn't he see the way Mattson looked at him? I could tell him for a fact that Mattson was not a nice guy. He could be straight–straight as a circle.

And he touched Nathan. Nathan, who even I know now, was scared of being touched. Unlike him, I saw the way he had flinched at contact and tried to get away.

Then he grabbed his wrist and I sort of...lost it.

That's when I realized I wanted to protect the weaker boy.

Speaking of which...

I jumped off my beanbag where I had been waiting and was about to run out the door if something didn't stumble into me first.

"What the hell?" I muttered. The black haired boy looked up and I stopped short at his crystal eyes. Shit, snap out of it. "You're late." I scolded, trying to keep myself even and neutral.

He leaned against the wall and nodded, rubbing his eyes. Something was wrong. His cheeks were pink and the circles under his eyes were dark, darker than usual. That was another thing. Since I met him, I've noticed he's always pale and looking exhausted.

"S–sorry." He whispered and shut his eyes as he began a horrible rack of coughing. He clutched the shirt covering his chest. I moved to put a hand on his shoulder but stopped short. "I...uh, got–"

He stumbled forward and I caught him in my arms. His forehead was burning and my concern rose considerably.

He jumped from my cool touch.

"Sorry!" He exclaimed. Then he shook his head fiercely as he moved around me. "I'm fine. Let's get–"

Then he collapsed.

.~*~. NATHAN .~*~.

I was in pain. My father was in front of me, and the hate in his eyes were evident. I looked at my bloodied hands to see they were small, like when I was ten. He had his belt and was screaming at me. I cried and cowered in the corner as he began slashing the leather. It stung my skin.

Then it stopped and another man came into view. Mr. Steven was going around the house, knocking everything over, dumping out the contents of the school bag and grinding it under his foot. He came over and grabbed my neck, hurling me against the opposite wall.

He came again and I screamed, begging for him to stop. He smiled sweetly and I saw his hand, coming for me, wanting desperately to clasp around my neck and strangle me breathless like my dad had done countless times before, and like in every one of those memories...

I screamed.

"Nathan, it's okay! It's only a dream. Wake up, you're safe." A voice reached my ears.

It's a dream. It's only a dream.

My dad was gone. But Mr. Stevens wasn't. He was a nightmare, my personal nightmare come to life. I had until the end of the month to summon fifteen hundred dollars, every month, for the rest of my life. And if I didn't...I began trembling at the thoughts of what could happen.

Then why was I dreaming? Why was I sleeping?

Where am I?

.~*~. RYDER .~*~.

He screamed. That snapped me out of my daze. I had been sitting at the edge of the bed, watching him sleep in the midst of a fever. I checked his temperature: 105 degrees.

He must have had a nightmare. He continued to thrash and claw at an invisible force. Tears streamed from his eyes and suddenly a dreadful scream escaped his dream.

I couldn't handle it anymore. I sat next to him and gathered him in my arms. I held him close until his trembling died down a notch, and brushed the soft black hair out of his moist face.

His tears did not cease.

He began murmuring to the people in his dream. "Please...stop. Don't hurt me. Please..."

Suddenly he whimpered and clutched his left wrist, curling into me.

I held him tighter and whispered, even when I knew he couldn't hear,

"I won't hurt you."

Chapter ~Eight~

I felt...safe.

The feeling was so foreign it was frightening.

My chest was burning and I was vaguely aware of my moist face. There was a soft light ready to greet me when my eyes opened, and it was warm, almost hot. I couldn't remember falling asleep last night. My fever had gotten worse and I could barely stay on my feet. Where was I now?

I forced my eyes to open. It seemed sealed shut from the tears that spilled over during the nightmare. Gosh, the nightmare. Sometimes it would last the entire night. I pushed it out of my mind for the moment, as I always did.

I felt something around me and I was confused. I opened my eyes completely.

What the heck?

I was curled up in a ball, with Ryder's arm holding me close. What was he doing? I began shaking. He was too close. Did he do something?

He groaned at my movement and began waking up. I squeezed my eyes shut so he would think I hadn't woken up yet. That would be awkward.

"Oh shit." I heard him mutter as he came to his senses. But for a moment he didn't move. I felt his eyes trained on the top of my head. His hand brushed the hair that had fallen in my face away.

I jumped and the trembles got worse.

"Fuck! I thought he stopped..."

He maneuvered so I rested on the pillows and scooted away. I relaxed a bit, but then he began shaking me lightly.

"Hey, wake up." He nudged my shoulder and I pretended to wake up.

I blinked my eyes open again. The light burst through the window on the side of the room, but Ryder's face filled my vision. Wait, I was still in his room? Had I fallen asleep?

"Where..." I whispered hoarsely. He seemed to relax slightly.

I felt a tickle in my chest and began coughing harshly. His faced crumpled with concern.

"Come on, you need medicine."

"I'm," A cough betrayed my words, "Fine."

"Fine my ass." I shuddered. "Shit, sorry. Aw, fuck...Geez!" He rambled and ruffled his hair. I pushed myself in a sitting position, getting as far as I could without falling off the bed. He seemed to notice and backed up.

"Sorry. You collapsed yesterday." He mumbled, trying to change the subject.

"I did?" I asked in disbelief. I've never collapsed before.

"You had a really high fever, nothing to worry about." He tried to reassure me. Why was he trying to help me? "But you do need medicine."

"No." I groaned and held my head in my hands. It hurt.

"Right, like you have a choice." He muttered. He pulled me off of the bed by my hand and I jumped away as soon as I was standing. I was being extra edgy this morning. The fever made me feel out of it and weak. Add last night's nightmare, and I was a wreck.

I followed him down the stairs and through the big house, knowing full well I couldn't really do anything else. He led me to a big kitchen and walked over to one of the cabinets. He found a pill bottle and popped the lid, shaking out a pill. He readied a glass of water and held it out. I looked at it doubtfully.

"Take it, you'll feel better." I took it carefully and dismissed the thought he was trying to poison me. "You can take another tonight, and you should start to feel better by tomorrow with rest."

Rest, sounds easy enough...wait, what?

"What time is it?" I jumped awake. He looked at his watch and said, "Half past one."

My eyes widened. "I missed school!"

"Yeah," He said annoyed, "Because of a 105 degree fever. I think you had the right to skip."

"That's nothing." I whispered to myself. Work started in about two hours. I can probably stop by home and take a shower before then.

I turned and left the kitchen. He followed asking, "Where are you going?"

"Home, I need to get ready for work." Where was his room with my bag?

He grabbed my hand in my haste. Honestly, I had no idea where I was going. "You are not going work. What if you collapse and are holding plates?"

"Not like I haven't fallen before." I muttered under my breath.

Apparently he heard because he pulled me to face him and said, "I'm sorry, I hadn't meant to bring those two to you, and certainly not to get you hurt. I also hadn't known about what they did to you at school. If I knew sooner, I would have stopped it."

I frowned. What did he mean? That he cared whether or not I was hurt?

"Why?" I asked. He shrugged and looked down, obviously showing he wasn't going to answer. Fine. I began walking through the house trying to find the stairs. Finally I found it near the front door and took it quickly.

"I'm not letting you go to work." He called as I found his room.

"I have to."

"No, you don't. Look at yourself!" I grabbed my bag and turned to leave but as soon as I turned he blocked my way and held my shoulders. "Stay here for the day and get rest and relax. I'm sure you can miss a couple days of work."

"No." My voice broke and my frame quivered. He noticed and looked at me worriedly. "I need the money. I'm more afraid of what will happen if I miss work than if I get a little sick."

He stared at me then dropped his hands. "Why do you need the money?"

I looked away.

"You're hiding something Nate."

Nate?

"Look at me."

I looked at my hand and began playing with my sleeve.

"You know what? You're not going to like it, but here it is. Inn going to take care of you. I'm going to listen to you and get you what you need. I'm going to help you, and you're going to trust me."

Chapter ~Nine~

He hid my bag. He hid it! Apparently he didn't trust me enough to not run when he wasn't looking. He called his mom, asking her to call Mrs. Clair to inform her I wasn't coming to work. His conversation sounded like this:

"Hi mom." He paused. "Um, can you call Mrs. Clair? Nathan has a high fever and he really shouldn't be working." There was a pause. "He's, uh, here with me. He stayed over last night cause he collapsed, and..." There was a rambling, muffled voice on the other end and Ryder's face turned red. "Mom!" He hissed. He glanced at me then away. "He just...no, he just needs to rest and I know he'll go to work if I'm not blocking him so...ew! Don't ever say that again!"

I frowned and when he hung up I asked, "What did she say?"

He smiled and said, "You don't want to know."

Oh...yeah, I probably don't. He forced me to sit across from him on the floor as he brought out his game controllers. He offered one and I shook my head. He shrugged and left it next to me. I held my knees close to my chest.

I've never had a friend before. There was no time for playing. Plus, I've never been in someone's house if I wasn't cleaning or tutoring. It felt weird not doing...anything.

"You need to relax." He muttered. "When was the last time you've played video games?"

I remember once, when I was little with my mom. "Nine years old."

His head snapped to face me in disbelief. "Okay, when did you last have fun?" He asked jokingly.

"Nine years old."

He paused the game and turned to me. "What happened when you were nine?"

I looked him in the eye. I owed him for helping me. I knew better than to leave things unpaid. But for some reason, that wasn't what made me say the words. There was something in his eyes that were different from before. "My mother died."

He leaned in close to catch my whisper. I looked down at my hands holding my knees and suddenly he was next to me, holding me in a tight hug. I jumped but didn't pull away.

"How?"

I sniffed my nose that had chosen to act strange. "I don't...know." I really didn't. She just seemed to disappear, but my dad's words stung my ears, "You're nobody! You're the reason she's gone!"

"Shit, you're crying!"

"What?" I raised a hand to my face to find it was true. "Sorry." I hid my face in my arms.

"No, no! It's okay." He wrapped his arms around me once again.

This made me confused. When his friends were around, he acted like I was nonexistent. Then why was he acting like this? And why was he hugging me?

"Why do you care?" I asked, pushing him off.

He was silent before he answered, "Because...I..." He didn't finish. I looked up at him from the side and he looked frustrated.

There was a knock on the door. Ryder muttered a, "Perfect timing" before getting up and answering.

"You." He asked narrowed his eyes.

"Mr. Kenneth." Said a voice just as cold. I got up and timidly looked around Ryder's shoulder.

"Hi Mattson." I said.

He looked genuinely surprised and replied, "Nathan? You're here already? You weren't at school."

"He was sick." Ryder answered in an indifferent expression. He eyed Mattson as if he were dangerous.

"Are you okay?" Mattson reached out to check my temperature and I jumped back. Ryder grabbed his hand in a flash.

There was a moment of silence as the two shot daggers at each other before Mattson broke the silence and said, "I just came by to tell you Mrs. Kenneth will be coming home late tonight, she is meeting with Mr. Kenneth."

"Got it." Ryder said shoving his hand away. "You can go."

He shut the door and sighed in frustration.

"You two don't seem to get along very well." I commented.

"We have our disagreements." He said offering me a glance.

"Oh..." I whispered and played with my left sleeve. I caught him staring at it. I closed my eyes sat on the bed. I was really tired. Maybe the medicine made me drowsy.

Next to me the bed sunk under Ryder's weight. "You can tell me, you know. On your own terms." I heard him say off handedly. I shook my head and leaned against the bedpost. Mrs. Clair, Kristy, and Mrs. Kenneth only know about my dad and some of what happened. No body knows about Mr. Stevens. I laughed a hollow laugh as I realized only girls know about me. They're too observant.

"Only girls? Then can I be the first guy?" My eyes snapped open and he laughed. "You spoke out loud."

My hand flew to my mouth and he laughed again. This is the first time I made him actually laugh. Usually I cause him too scoff and roll his eyes.

"Hey!" He said suddenly. I looked up wearily. "Want to go to the park?"

"I thought I was too sick." I said. If I had time to waste at the park, I might as well go to work. He rolled his eyes and grabbed my hand, pulling me down the stairs and soon we were out the door walking down the street. I looked up at the sky. It was overcast. Great, what if it started raining and I got a cold? Would he force me to skip school and work again?

"Relax." He said, putting an arm around me.

"Stop doing that." I said trying to shake him off.

He smirked. "Can't help it."

.~*~. RYDER .~*~.

He was so cute. Or something. He looked at the playground like it was foreign. He sat in a swing and I next to him. We were less awkward now, thank god I finally got my shit together. He doubtfully kicked off the ground. I know what he was thinking: he'd rather be working than be here.

I laughed. He didn't really have a choice.

It was kind of cold and I prayed it didn't rain. The wind brushed his hair out of his face, and for a moment he looked content. It reminded me of when he woke up this morning.

I was so glad he hadn't woken up before me. That would have been embarrassing. His cheeks were tinged pink from the fever and he was still trembling. But it only reminded me how fragile he was despite how much he did for himself.

Though, knowing why he was so fragile would help.

I want to know why there are scars on his wrist. I want to know why he trembles when being touched or when someone curses. I want to protect him from what can hurt him.

An image of Mattson looking at him crossed my mind and I forced it away.

I looked at him and almost fell off my swing. He was smiling. And this time, it wasn't fake but authentic.

"Is this your first time on a swing or something?"

"First time since my mom passed away." He said and I caught the brief pain that flashed across his eyes.

"What about your dad?"

He stopped swinging and looked down. His hands clutched the metal chains. "He's gone too." He whispered.

Shit. "Sorry, I really shouldn't have asked. It must've been hard."

He shook his head and I saw his frame begin to shake. I thought there would be silence, so when he continued speaking I was shocked.

"It was a relief, kind of." He took a deep breath and swayed on the swing. His voice was so quiet I could barely hear. "He was abusive after mom left. Then one day..." He rubbed the inside of his wrist and suddenly I knew where this was going.

"No way...did he do that to you?" I asked in disbelief. He nodded slowly.

"He killed himself after."

His eyes were filled with sadness and pain. What kind of father does that? What kind of kid has to live through that?

"Then who do you live with?"

He only shook his head, indicating he was alone. That's terrible. What was it like to go home everyday, and know there was no body to greet you? Then wake up in a completely empty house?

"How long have you...?"

"Since I was eleven. I began working when I was thirteen."

"Why? Students shouldn't work when they're that young. Aren't there services that are supposed to look out for you?"

He was silent as I watched him think of what to say. Half of me wanted to know what more there could be, the other half wanted nothing more to have happened.

"There's this man." He began in a whisper. "My dad borrowed a lot of money from him for...stuff. When my dad killed himself, that man found me. He handled everything. I have to– had to pay back the entire loan in my fathers place."

My eyes were the size of saucers. "How much?" I murmured.

He answered, "A lot."

"Is that why you took the job? The reason you work so much?"

He nodded. I felt like finding this guy and beating the crap out of him. How could he make Nathan go through this? Look at him! Mom told me all he does is work and go to school. He doesn't have a life.

He wasn't finished. "Every month I had to make the payday. If I didn't–"

"What?" I asked through clenched teeth.

He shut his eyes and clutched his head.

"...nevermind. I'm fine. It's all in the past. It doesn't happen anymore, I swear. I'm only paying for rent and living expenses now. It doesn't happen anymore. It...it..."

I get off my but and kneel in front of him. I reach up and hold him until his trembles cease.

"You can still tell me. What did he do Nathan?"

His voice cracked, and for a moment I found it hard to believe that this was the boy who hid his life from everybody. That this was the boy who forces a smile everyday at work.

"Anything he wanted."

Chapter ~Ten~

~*~. RYDER .~*~.

●

I was going to kill him. I was going to strangle the breath out of this man that caused pain to my Nate. If Nathan hadn't been shaking in fear, shaking from those memories, I would have tracked down this man and made him regret every little thing he has done. But I didn't. Why?

The heavens chose that time to make it rain.

I began freaking out because he was getting soaked and he was already sick to begin with. I cursed for not bringing a jacket and made a spur of the moment decision. I stripped off my shirt and held it above his head. He laughed at my attempt, because he obviously had no care for his health. But the laugh was forced.

If the rain hadn't begun pouring, I would be steaming with anger. I was just about to grab him, hold him close. I can't believe he told me...anything. Everything. I can't believe what he'd been through. I can't believe I hadn't been there earlier to protect him. I can't believe I had been about to cry.

So, using it as an excuse, I held him close as we ran back to the house, so the rain wouldn't affect him as much, and so I could reassure myself he was safely in my arms and not in someone else's. When we got through the door he shook his head and looked down at himself.

"Are you trying to get me sick?" He asked and shivered from the cold.

"Come on, you can borrow my clothes."

I looked at him through my peripherals and caught him look away from my body, blushing. I smirked, feeling giddy knowing I was the cause of the blush. I know I'm hot and got muscle. I'm glad he noticed too.

I grabbed a T-shirt that was obviously going to be too big and some stretchy soccer shorts.

He looked at the shirt and gripped his wrist. Come to think of it, I've only ever seen him in long sleeves, even when it was hot. The reason he wore long sleeves must be to hide his wrist.

"I know now." I reassured and handed the shirt over. "You don't have to hide it."

He nodded slowly and accepted it before going into the bathroom.

I changed out of my jeans for some sweats. I had just pulled on a clean shirt when there was a crash from inside the bathroom.

My heart jumped and I began pounding on the door. "Nathan, what was that? Are you okay?"

"Uh..." He voice came through as a muffle. "It's nothing, I...fell..."

He fell? Was he dizzy? "I'm coming in." I pushed the door open all the way and looked for him. He was sprawled on the ground with his head resting on the cabinet. He had the pants on but seemed to have fallen before he could put on a shirt. He held his head and groaned.

"My head." He stated. I hurriedly picked him up and brought him to the bed, pulling the covers over his slim frame.

"What–" But stopped short when I saw his back and front. The scars stood out from his pale skin. Some had begun to fade while recent bruises marked his stomach.

Anger flared up like a torch. It took all my effort to keep calm and focus on the matter at hand.

"I'll be right back with some medicine, don't go anywhere."

With his eyes closed he laughed as I left and even if it was hollow, it sounded sweet.

.~*~. NATHAN .~*~.

I hadn't meant to fall, but my head made everything in my vision swim in pairs. When he came in, all I could think about was that he could see my scars. No one has ever seen it, save Mr. Stevens of course.

I shivered involuntarily knowing he was getting closer to me than anyone has my entire life, on top of that it all happened in one day. Thank god I caught myself earlier. If I had really shared that this was all still happening, I wouldn't be able to face him. I'd probably disgust him.

I thought about when we were running back to the house. For some reason, he cared more about blocking the rain than getting wet. I had unwillingly admitted to myself he had a really, unfairly, toned body.

I thought again about the times he held and comforted me. No one has ever done that. It felt...nice. For whatever reasons, someone cared about me, and what I've been through and if I'm hurt. He wasn't disgusted.

As I became drowsier and closed my eyes, I felt a smile tug it's way across my lips and I hid in the soft pillows.

Yeah, being with him wasn't so bad.

Did that mean...

"Mr. Ken-" The low voice stopped abruptly. I heard footsteps slowly enter the room. I didn't need to open my eyes to know it was Mattson. I was thankful Ryder had covered me before he left, because I knew he was staring down at me and I would die if anyone else saw the scars.

I felt his hand brush the side of my face and I forced myself to stay still and pretend to be asleep.

"If you so much as touch him I swear I'll kick your fucking white ass." Ryder's voice boomed.

I opened my eyes ever so slightly to see what was going on. Ryder just entered with some pills and a water bottle in hand. Mattson turned to meet him and smiled slyly.

"I didn't think you were the type to move this fast. I wouldn't thought you would date him before take him to-"

"He's sick." Ryder seethed with a fuming expression. "And I would never do that to him."

Do what?

"Isn't he adorable when he sleeps?" Mattson seemed to mock.

I saw his hand again but Ryder's voice stopped him. "Don't you fucking touch him Taylors. I swear, if you-"

"Fine." Mattson held up his hands in defense and laughed. "I'm not the one he needs protection from."

"You're the very person I plan on keeping him from." Ryder sneered and moved so he was between the two of us. "Now get the fuck out."

"As you wish, Mr. Kenneth. And your mother called again, she said Nathan may stay for the night if he wants." He smirked.

"Get out."

The door closed soon after and I knew he had left. Ryder faced me and sat on the edge of the bed. He shook me and I pretended to wake up.

"Take this." He shook out a pill and I downed it with the water.

"Thanks." I muttered sitting up. I glowered at myself. "I'm so much trouble, I know. Sorry."

"You're not trouble." I saw him glance down at my shirtless torso and look away with a blush.

I caused him to blush?

I scratched my head and pretended to be confused. "I thought I heard Mattson's voice."

He clenched his hands. "Yeah, my mom called to tell me something. How are you feeling?"

Fine, I thought. But what were they talking about? It sounded like I had been their main topic, but why would they be talking about me?

"Better." I felt extremely self-conscious of my scars and uselessly hid under the comforter.

He laughed. "What are you doing?"

"You saw."

There was silence before, "Yeah."

The weight holding down the bed disappeared and he came back, stuffing the shirt he had given me under the comforter.

"Thanks." I mumbled before slipping it on and pushing off the thick sheets.

I felt so weak right now. This entire day proved that sometimes I couldn't handle everything, and it sucked having it rubbed in my face. Yes, I was alone with nobody as support, but I've toughed it out through three years of work, sickness, bullying, school, and Mr. Stevens. It scared me in ways I couldn't think about, but I did it all on my own. Suddenly I meet Ryder, and in less than a week he already knows more than everybody else.

I rubbed my wrist and he sat down in front of me. "Your turn." He said.

"My turn...?"

"You told me your secrets. You're free to ask me anything you want."

Okay...like what? "Um, in that case...why are you dumb?"

He hung his head and laughed. "Really should have expected that. I just tend to fall behind in math. And other subjects."

"But why take advanced math if you can't do it?"

"Do you know anything about athletes? I can't do college with just sports alone. I can do it, as long as you help me." He smiled and I found myself caught. Or, it felt that way. I don't know why.

Then I remembered something. "What does the f-word mean?"

"Fuck?"

I winced. "No." I pulled on the sleeves that wouldn't go past my elbow. "The one everyone calls me."

He thought for a moment and moments later he remembered. "Oh, you mean fag?" He said softly. I nodded. He raised an eyebrow. "You don't know what it means but people call you that every day?"

I shrugged. "I just thought it was another insult. Does it have another meaning?"

"You're suddenly not as smart as I thought you were." I watched him carefully as a small smile tugged at his lips. "It means queer."

"Queer?" I asked. Meaning, gay?

Oh.

AN: SHORT BREAK! Thoughts? Thoughts?

Chapter ~Eleven~

"I'm not like that." I said feeling a flush creep up my cheeks.

He laughed. "I know."

"Why would they call me that?"

He shifted uncomfortably. "Well, could be because you look cute. Doesn't mean you're gay, but maybe Jonah's the weirdo with a complex and limited vocabulary."

"But–"

"It's just a word. They call everyone they dislike fags." I nodded slowly. "So, if you're not gay, got any girls in mind?" He asked with a slight smile. But there was something strange in his eyes, as if he wanted me to answer no.

Then again, no was the truth. "I've never had time for relationships."

He blinked and asked, "You've never had a girlfriend?" I shook my head. Maybe I was imagining it, but he looked like he was smiling and about to laugh and my zero love life.

"Oh." Was all he said.

.~*~. RYDER .~*~.

Hell yeah. Alright boys, my chances aren't zero and that's enough for me.

All he does is work. He literally doesn't have time for a life. All because of his messed up situation. Maybe my chances are zero after all.

But, if he's never had a girlfriend, and never even thought about a girl in that way, i can at least see how he feels about me, as a person of course. Nothing more. "You know you just might be gay."

Aw, cute. He blushed. "I—no, I'm not." He stuttered.

"You sure?" I smirked. "Have you ever looked at a guy in that way?"

He shook his head, obviously embarrassed.

Well, time to find out.

.~*~. NATHAN .~*~.

He had this sly smile. I felt my face grow warm. Why was he looking at me as if I was amusing? What was he thinking?

Suddenly he leaned forward and I couldn't back up any further when I hit the backboard. He crawled over between my legs and brushed my cheek.

I jumped and tried to push him away. What was he doing?

I knew my face was red and my heartbeat became quick. I shrunk back as he leaned forward and rested his forehead against mine.

Mr. Steven was in the back of my mind and I shut my eyes, but Ryders hand cupped my face, and all I could think of was how warm the room got, and he said, "Are you sure you're not?" Not...? He brushed the hair out of my face and I winced at his cold touch. He paused and spoke, "Sorry. Listen, I'm not going to hurt you."

I believed him. Aren't you feeling relieved a little too quickly, Nathan?

He smirked as he pulled away, pulling me with him, and turned so we were lying down and not sitting against the headboard. He leaned down, and I couldn't manage anything other than a whimpered, "Stop."

So he did. He looked at me in the eye and smiled. He knew I said stop not because I didn't like it, but because I had no idea what was happening.

He went back and I pushed myself up. I placed a hand over my chest. My heart was going wild.

What the heck? "What was that?" I asked a little feverish.

He shrugged. "Just wondering if you were really straight." Before I could say anything, he continued, "If that got your heart racing...anyway, how about some food? I'm starving."

He held open the door and I followed in a daze. And confusion. What just happened here?

What...uh...does that mean he's...

"If you're wondering how I swing, I have absolutely nothing against homosexuals, in fact..." He shook his head and laughed.

What? Was I the only one completely confused about what he was saying?

—

—

I kept my distance from him and kept an eye out as well. Maybe he was just teasing me, taking advantage of my sickness and keeping me in his house.

"When can I go home?"

"When you're better. Mom said you could stay over tonight."

"I'm better." I muttered.

He smiled slightly. "I know the difference between a fever flush and a cute blush. Eat your sandwich."

I looked down at the packed sandwich that would surely keep me going for at least two days. I took a bite and it was delicious.

"We'll probably have this again for dinner, or noodles since that's all I can make. Mom will be home late."

"I can cook." I offered. I've always cooked, my whole life.

"Oh, right." He nodded then put down his food. "You can get started if you want, everything's in the cabinets. I'm going to take a shower."

I nodded in agreement. He left and and I could finally breathe properly. I decided to multitask and eat while cooking. The cabinets were stocked with high priced items I would not have been able to use if I had not worked at the café.

Something simple. Chicken? I got everything from the freezer and pantry and proceeded to heating the stove with a pot above, making the barbecue chicken.

"Smells amazing." A low voice said from behind. I turned around. Mattson leaned against the doorframe watching me.

"Just making dinner while Ryder's in the shower." I said. He detached himself and looked over the pot, pushing against me. He really has a different sense of personal space.

"Lucky." He muttered and smiled. "May I help? I was just about to head home, but I'd love to stay a bit longer."

"Are you sure?" I asked.

He nodded. "That's what friends are for."

Friends. I don't have friends. There's no time, yet is Mattson one? Kristy is one, and the very few adults, I guess.

I thought of Ryder. Is he my friend? I don't think he thinks of me like that. But then why did he...God, I've never been more confused in my life.

"Can I ask you something?" I say.

"Sure." I had given him the job of stirring the pot and he stopped, putting the glass lid over the pot and turning to me. I leaned against the counter and dried my wet hands.

"Have you ever...liked someone?" I asked stupidly. What am I, an elementary schooler?

"Liked someone?" A small smirk played his lips as he looked at me. "Yeah."

"How do you know when you like them?" I asked and played with the hand towel.

"Well, when you think about them all the time. When they are near, you get nervous and your heart races into the sunset." He says dramatically. I laughed a little and he looked at me, suddenly serious. "When all you want is to be with them."

I nodded, and then shook my head. Could I...for Ryder? I thought about him, yes, most of the time as a bipolar idiot. My heart certainly began to race when he leaned in close. And I felt safe being with him today.

Suddenly Mattson closed the space and I was pushed against the counter. He grabbed my right hand and held me still.

"W...what are you...?" Uncomfortably I tried to evade his face but he let himself settle in the crook of my neck.

"When all you want to do," He murmured in my neck. It sent a chill down my spine. I didn't like it. "Is touch them."

His other hand traced my jaw and held it as he kissed underneath. He pushed himself against me and I was too shocked to say anything. His hand left my face, trailed down to my waist and followed slowly under my shirt.

"Sto...st–" His kissed the corner of my mouth just as my back arched from his touch on my back. He pushed himself against me and I felt caught, but in a different way. I felt him smile against my skin and he whispered, "And all I want to do is make you mine." His breath was centimeters away from colliding with my own.

My left hand moved desperately for something to use to push him away, resting for a moment too long on the hot burner.

I cried in pain and pulled away, holding my hand to my chest. He tried to look at the burn but I kept it fiercely to myself. Maybe if it were my right hand I'd allow him to help. But it was my left, and there was something I'd rather him not see right below my hand.

"Let me see, are you okay?" He tried again and I turned completely so he had no chance.

I felt tears prick my eyes and I shut it. A few stupid tears failed to stay hidden and escaped down my cheek. Ugh, I was crying. I hate myself. This is so annoying. P

"What the hell did you do?" Ryder yelled as he stormed into the kitchen. He was shirtless with an enraged expression. I turned sheepishly to look at him and he did a double take. Yeah yeah, I'm crying, whatever.

I gasped when he turned and punched Mattson in the face.

Then he put a protective arm around me and brought me in, where his other hand carefully took hold of my own to examine the burn.

"What did he do? How bad does it hurt?" He whispered.

"I'm fine." I croaked. He ran a light finger over a tender spot and I shut my eyes.

"Go." He said in a dark voice full of venom at Mattson. "Don't you ever touch or come near him again. I swear I've said that more than once already."

Mattson backed away and left, not before he raised his eyebrows at me, giving this loaded look. Ryder saw and his fists bunched. I shied away into his arms and hid my face.

"Hey, it's not that bad." He whispered soothingly as he pulled my hand under the cold running water. "It might sting for a while though."

I nodded and allowed him to inspect the slight burn. I've been getting hurt a lot lately. On top of that, I'm not working or going to school!

"What was he doing?" Ryder asked gently as he grabbed some ice and put it in a bag, wrapping a cloth around it and pressing it against my fingers.

"Nothing."

"Yeah right." He grabbed my chin and made me look into his eyes. "What did he do?"

For a moment I couldn't respond because of how sincere and deep his grey eyes were. I opened my mouth and closed it again. I had a feeling if I told him anything, he would get upset. But he was already upset, and he looked like he would die if he didn't know. His curiosity really is the worst.

"He...um," I gulped and looked away feeling my face heat up. "He touched me...a little bit." His eyes grew dark and I quickly added. "But...he was just..." I trailed off, realizing I didn't really know what he had been doing.

"Why did he do that?"

"I was asking him..." Oh great. I was asking him to clarify my feelings for Ryder. I couldn't tell him that.

"Ask him?"

I gave up and mumbled, "How you know when you like someone." He looked a little shock but regained his composure and nodded for me to continue. "Uh, then he answered. And, um, then he got a little too close, and began..." I shuddered and shook my head.

"That fuckin' bast–" He cut off when he looked at me and gave a lame smile. "Never mind."

I looked at the door he escaped through, and thought; I don't think he wants to be just my friend. I shivered again despite the sting in my hand and realized the friendship we had, had pretty much vanished.

Chapter ~Twelve~

He made me stay overnight. I thought he was going too far and it was unnecessary but he insisted. Twice throughout the darkening afternoon, I caught him staring at me. He would look away and pretend he wasn't. It really made me confused, and a bit self-conscious, but I tried my best to ignore it.

He threw a bundle of oversize clothes at me. "Um, go take a shower." I nodded but half way across the room he stopped me by the arm. He smirked and added, "Don't fall this time."

Wouldn't that be an interesting situation?

I escaped the moment by rushing into the bathroom. I felt really weird. I pushed those feelings aside and hurried to get in and out of the shower. It felt nice– everything was nice here. Considering the standards I lived by, I was really setting the bar low. Speaking of which, the bill should go down since I haven't been using any electricity back at the house. I smiled and pulled on Ryder's shirt. It was way too big, but did nothing whatsoever to fool anyone of my thin frame. I left the bathroom to find he wasn't in the room.

I threw the clothes I was using in the hamper by his dresser and laid back on the bed.

I felt my eyes droop. How can I be tired? I slept so much! I couldn't still be sick; I took actual medicine and ate actual meals, and had actual sleep. I had been actually cared for. I better not fall into this routine, otherwise it would be hard to start back with work.

Mrs. Stevens smirking face lingered at the edge of mind...

It's decided then. Tomorrow, I'm going back to work.

.~*~. RYDER .~*~.

"Oh honey, I knew things were hard for him, I didn't know it was like that!"

I nodded silently on the other side of the phone. I called mom and informed her the basics about Nate. Huh, Nate. That's cute. Wait, don't get distracted.

Apparently, she knew he lived alone and worked as much as he could pay off some bills and stuff. I told her a bit about the debt, and she got worked up. I didn't tell her what the man did to Nathan before. She would blow up. Literally, explode.

"You really like Nathan, don't you?" She taunted on the other end. Seriously, sometimes she just doesn't act her age. She knew about my sexual preference, and sometimes it got really annoying. "I knew you'd like him. That's why I took you to that café in the first place–"

"Wait, you were setting me up?" I asked in bewilderment. "Mom!" I knew she had a reason for taking me there, but not...

"It's okay, no need to thank me."

"Mom!" Then I lowered my voice. "Geez...how do you even know him?"

"I do go to the café a lot, but I also knew his parents."

His parents? I felt my eyes grow heavy. "They died."

I heard her sigh. "Yeah. We were good friends. When his mother, Molly, died, I hadn't known his father had grown abusive. Not until..."

She trailed off. "Not until?"

"Not until he decided to end both his and his sons life."

She knew about that too? Was I the only one that hadn't known? "He told me about that." I felt myself smile a bit. "He trusted me enough to show me his scars–including his wrists."

There was silence before a loud squeal erupted on the other end. "He trusts you! Okay, I better go now. Remember, use protection."

"Mom!"

"Bye honey!"

How can she say that? To her son?

I ended the call and sighed, then laughed a little. I had the best mom in the world, though I'll never admit it. I walked back to my room wondering if he was out of the shower yet. When I opened the door I found him curled up on the bed, breathing soundly.

I thought of when I saw him at the café when I went with Jonah and Marcus. The way they insulted him, and he just took it, keeping his façade up so his job would be saved. He acted strong, but he was so vulnerable and...

I shook my head. No, he's strong, period. I turned and was about to head to my closet but tripped on my school bag. I swore as I hit the ground. Damn it...

His eyes fluttered open and he sat up a bit. He looked drowsy and a little flushed.

"Did...you just trip over a bag?"

I rolled my eyes and got up. "Shut up."

He looked at me for a moment, his blue eyes dark in this light. God, he was so cute the way he looked at me. Oh great...he was turning me from bi to completely gay.

"What?" I asked.

He blushed deeply and shook his head, looking away. I felt a grin cross my face. I made him blush.

"What?" I asked again and walked over. The grin was full blown with amusement. I leaned closely and he jumped and blinked. He looked confused as he looked to the side, anywhere but my eyes. Hmm, I wonder what he was thinking.

"Uh..." He mumbled.

"Yes?"

He opened then closed his mouth. He scooted a bit back and I sat at the edge. "What's up?"

"Nothing." He stuttered. Nothing my ass.

He seemed deep in thought, and confused. What could he be thinking? I knew he wasn't going to tell me. He could be a good liar when he wanted to be, unless I'm paying attention.

Nathan had a strong façade. He worked like his life depended on it. He went to school and toughed out through fevers and colds so he wouldn't fall behind. But every month, it wouldn't make a difference. He was turned and proven to be weak, and completely unable to do anything, against anyone.

As I looked at him now, I felt my needs to hold him rise.

As long as he will have me, I was going to protect him.

I crawled over and nudged him so he had no choice but to fall back, lying down under me. His face was a bright red, and I know it wasn't because of a fever.

I leaned down completely and gently pressed my lips against his.

.~*~. NATHAN .~*~.

What was he...why was he...what?

——

He pulled away. I could only stare wide-eyed. For a moment he stared back, before his face turned to utter shock.

"Shit." He gasped but he didn't move. He stared at me, with his hair falling just past his face.

I felt my face grow warm. My hands checked my cheeks, just to see if a fever was present. But it didn't feel like a fever, not at all.

"Ryder?" I whispered. He locked his eyes with my own. I opened my mouth to speak but shut it quickly. I was confused about a lot of things at the moment, but one thing was for sure.

We kissed. Like our lips touched. That was amiss right?

My hand covered my mouth and I looked away embarrassed. He just kissed me. Ryder just kissed me.

"I–I didn't...I mean, uh..." He stuttered. He ran a hand through his hair. "I'm sorry, I couldn't...I couldn't help it. You just..."

He shut up before he could say anything stupid. He was silent as he sorted his thoughts, and I wondered what he was thinking when a smile appeared on his lips.

"Do you mind?" I asked quietly. He rushed to move away so he wasn't directly on top of me.

Okay, think Nathan. Ryder just...kissed you. What was I supposed to think? What was I supposed to say? The warmth it brought and the strange feathery sensation it gave was nothing like I've ever felt before. But why was it Ryder that was giving me these feelings?

It didn't feel wrong. I looked at him nervously, wondering again what he was thinking. He stared back as if I would be the first one to break the silence.

He cleared his throat. "So...uh, we should be getting to sleep." He looked anywhere but my face.

What, was he going to pretend like that didn't happen?

I felt a little hurt when I thought this. Maybe he didn't like it, or I had done something wrong.

Wait, why was I disappointed? I shouldn't be. Ryder just made a mistake. He was confused and distracted with whatever he was thinking, and made a small mistake. And I...perhaps I'm gay, or bi, considering I haven't looked at a girl that way either. But if I was, wouldn't I be proving Jonah and Marcus correct?

That I'm a f...

Wow, I can't even think that word.

Ryder pulled off his shirt. I felt my eyes grow slightly wider. Why couldn't I have even a bit of muscle? I felt relieved knowing he was keeping his baggy shorts on as he flipped off the light and climbed into bed.

Bed?

Well, I guess we did share the bed last night. This was nothing. Absolutely nothing...

Again, why did I feel disappointed?

No! I wasn't disappointed!

He faced away, to one wall, and I faced the other.

"About...what just happened," He whispered quietly. I stayed still, but my heart decided to pick up the pace. "I'm sorry."

He was apologizing? Did that mean it was a mistake?

I felt the breath I had been holding leave my lungs and my eyelids drooped. Of course it was a mistake. Who in their right mind would like me, the messed up kid with no family, no friends, and tons of problems?

"For not asking I mean. That wasn't cool of me. Im sorry but I don't regret it. Good night Nathan."

Chapter ~Thirteen~

.~*~. NATHAN .~*~.

But I don't regret it. Whatever he meant, I would have to think about it later. Right now, I was faced with the task of getting out of bed. Somehow, we had ended up just a tad bit tangled. Without waking him I moved his arms away from my waist and got up. I hurriedly put on the clothes I had been wearing when I came here a couple days ago, that he had washed, and was now in search of my bag.

He put it on a shelf.

Where I couldn't reach it.

That was not fair.

I brought over the chair from his desk and was just able to brush my fingers against the strap. I jumped and the bag tumbled off to the ground. It crashed with a loud thud, but somehow, he didn't wake up. Wow, he was a heavy sleeper.

I decided I might as well leave a note for him when he wakes up, just in case he freaked out. It read, "Going to work. Can't stop me. Thank you. Bye." It was quite heartfelt.

I felt amazing. That had been the most sleep I've ever gotten, and the most food I've ever consumed. I felt refreshed and ready to take on extra hours. Plus, I woke up early so I can get a shift in before school started. Another plus, today was Friday.

I practically ran to the café. I wonder if Kristy had needed to work extra because I wasn't there. Admittedly, I feel kind of bad about that. I usually did most of the work, and she rarely came in, in the mornings.

So I was quite surprised when she attacked me as I entered the back room.

"Where in the name of cake have you been? Do you know how worried I was? Did something happen? Oh my god, don't tell me you got jumped by a hobo. I checked your school, your house, your–"

"You know where I live?" I asked a little stunned.

She snorted. "Of course I do. I'm your best friend. Don't change the subject. Where were you? Are you okay?" She was jumping and tugging on my arm as if I was dead. But, that was a little impossible, considering I was standing right here.

"I'm fine." I smiled at her for added affect. "I was sick, and Ryder made me skip work and school."

"Ryder?" She asked in disbelief. "I thought he was evil. Good, I should thank him for keeping you...where exactly?"

"His house."

"For keeping you at his...house...he let you stay at his house?" She screamed the last part. I seriously have no clue why she seemed excited.

"Why are you screaming?"

She shrugged. "I don't know. I guess that's just news to me. I didn't think he was...nice. Or that you knew how to make friends. Did anything happen?"

My mind treaded back to the night before, then the afternoon before, and all the way from when I woke up...I decided to ignore it. Ignore everything. It will only end up confusing me.

"Nothing."

She notched an eyebrow and asked slowly, "Oh really?"

"What?"

"Something happened, didn't it?"

"Honestly, what could happen? It's not like he beat me up."

Though, he did get a bit personal. I wasn't going to tell her that. But the way she looked at me right now told me she was second-guessing my words. Kristy really was my best friend. She pretty much knew me better than myself, and has always known me. Sometimes she acted like a complete girl whenever she announced she was going on a date, or like a lazy bum whenever it came to work, or like a protective sister whenever it came to me.

"Okay, he didn't beat you up." She nodded really slowly. "So what did he do?"

"Um, nothing?"

"Nathan."

The face she gave broke me, and I started, "He−" Before I was interrupted by Mrs. Clair.

"You're back, how are you feeling?"

"Better, much better." I answered with a smile, thankful for the interruption.

"Are you sure you want to start work so—"

"I'm sure." With that I glanced at Kristy, mouthing, 'later' before heading out to the front.

An hour later, I was rushing out of the café toward school. When I said 'later', I meant after school later, or maybe even the next day. Or never! Yeah, I'll go with never.

"Nathan!" I whipped my head around alarmingly fast as I entered school grounds. No one ever talked to me or offered a glance, I was invisible, so the only possibilities were Mattson, someone I was jumpy just thinking about, and Jonah, someone I really wasn't in the mood for.

"What is this?" I turned around and came to face to face with Ryder. Wait, he was at school...and talking to me...I don't know why, but even after those strange things he said last night, I expected him to revert back to the jerk he seemed to be during school.

"What's what?" I asked him a little confused.

He looked a little annoyed and irritable as he stuck out his hand, holding a paper with careless scribbles. It was the note I left him before leaving.

"What about it?"

"Can't stop me? Really?" He shook his head and laughed a little. "So you went to work this morning?"

"Yeah, I need to work to get paid." He stared at me without giving much emotion away. Why does it feel like he I glanced around awkwardly before asking, "What?"

"Nothing. You're still coming over to tutor me, right?" Well, someone sounded eager. I guess he finally felt like bringing his grades up.

"Sure. I'll see you later then." I nodded and began walking toward the building. I was a little nervous. Jonah and Markus always seem to find me first thing in the morning. Ryder tapped my shoulder to stop me. "Yeah?"

"I wont let anyone hurt you, okay?"

We stood there staring at each other as I did my best to sustain normal breaths. I nodded once and hurried toward the building, only pausing momentarily inside to catch my breath.

Something is seriously wrong with me.

Maybe I should just...avoid him?

I made my way quickly to class hoping nothing will happen. Luckily, nothing did! It was a huge surprise.

But I did see Jonah eye me during class. It was a simple enough gesture that told me to watch my back.

Great.

Then Ryder walked in. He searched around the class expectantly, and smiled in my direction. I looked around me just in case it was someone else, not believing he was openly...I don't know, making contact?

Then the unexpected happened. Jonah waved him over but he shook his head, instead walking over and taking the seat next to me. Everyone's focus was on him. Go figure, over the last week, I've been paying enough attention to summarize that he was liked by all. Apparently, compared to everyone else, he was smart. On top of being athletic and good looking, he was every girls dream.

...Did I just say good looking?

Well, I guess he was. Objectively speaking. I gave a barely perceptive side-look from the corner of my eyes and looked at his face, that was directed forward to his aunt. His blond hair had grown out a bit so it reached his ears, and was gelled slightly around his face. His grey eyes we re...admittedly, really nice...and seemed happier than normal, like a silent joke was going on that only he knew. He smiled pleasantly up at the lesson being written on the board as if he actually understood–or was pretending to– unlike his usual arrogant manner.

"Maybe you should pay attention to Ms. Richmond, I'll need you to explain all of this later." He whispered softly.

Shoot, was I staring? I felt my face heat up despite the cold air-con and I focused my attention toward the board.

Five minutes later, my face was still warm.

He sighed and shifted so he was slouching, and moved his leg so it brushed next to mine.

Focus, Nathan! Why is he distracting you?

"...Ryder, and Nathan."

My head jerked up, what did I miss? Am I in trouble? I can't be in trouble. I just came back.

"This should be...interesting." He whispered.

"What? What did she say?"

"Did you have other things on your mind?" He smirked.

My face began to warm up, and I decided to save myself and speak what I was thinking an hour before getting distracted, "Only how fast I'll need to run to get to my next class."

His smirk fell a bit. "I won't–"

"Ryder, Nathan, are you paying attention?"

My head snapped to the front and I nodded at Ms. Richmond. "Sorry."

She smiled a bit and continued. "It will be due at the end of the quarter. Most of what we do in class and that is assigned will help you. I'll pass some papers around that explains what criteria needs to be covered."

She began passing around papers and I nudged Ryder. "What did she say before?"

"We're starting a project. Hell if I know what it's about. There are three people per group, guess who's my partner?"

"Are you looking at him?"

He smiled. A perfect smile, I noticed. Not like how I smiled, not at all. Even at the café, I could tell when it doesn't reach my eyes.

"What's wrong?"

"Nothing." I said quietly and turned my attention to the paper that had been passed out. There were a lot of theories we had to cover and it may take a while. At least we already are studying together.

"Wait!" I whisper shouted and turned to him. "Did you say three people?"

Ryder shrugged. "Yeah."

"Who else is with us?"

"Um, Marcus?"

I laid my head on the desk. "Fantastic."

"Don't worry. Marcus isn't a bad guy. He's just a push over around Jonah. I've known him forever. He's cool, the entire team would rather band with him instead of Jonah if he spoke up from time to time."

I shook my head. "Ryder..."

"He won't hurt you. Neither will Jonah." His eyes darkened. "Or Mattson." He added as an afterthought.

When did Mattson come into our conversation?

"Why–"

"Talking about me?" A voice came from in front of us. My head snapped up to stare up at a Mattson standing casually. I just noticed that the class was getting up and breaking into groups.

Ryder stiffened next to me. I can tell, because his leg was still really close.

"We weren't." I said, mostly because it was true and we hadn't been. I almost forgot he was in this class. The sight of him made me a little nervous. I felt vulnerable.

He nodded before leaning slightly on the desk. He leaned closely to whisper in my ear. "Looks like you two are getting close." I jumped at his nearness, yes, jumped, as in off the chair. I landed on my back.

He smirked a little before shaking his head. "Later Nathan."

A couple kids who happened to look at that moment laughed before turning back to their own conversations. I felt a little sad, knowing Mattson seemed like a completely different person now. Not as friendly as before.

"I'm going to kill him." Ryder seethed. He offered a hand that I took and got up.

"It's my fault, probably." Right?

He turned to me. "It is not your fault. Don't think that."

Huh, okay? Someone cleared their throat loud enough for us to notice and we looked to the new person standing to the side.

Marcus.

His gaze shifted from the floor to Ryder to me then back to the floor. He looked extremely awkward. Come on Nathan, it's for a grade.

"Okay then, grab a chair and we'll see what this project is." I said quietly.

He shrugged and brought over a chair to sit at our desk.

The rest of the period was spent reading the packet. We had to make a presentation explaining the theories, along with having to pass this test at the end. Apparently, if we don't pass, it drops our grades down a letter. Little words were shared, so when the bell finally rang, I rushed to stuff everything in my bag and be on my way.

Ryder was still in the class as I headed toward my next period, when I hear my name. "Nathan wait!"

I turned and eyed Marcus wearily.

I didn't say anything. Ryders words earlier made it seem like he's not completely evil, but I didn't want any trouble.

He took a deep breath and spoke quickly. "I'm sorry."

What?

"I'm sorry for every time I hit, kicked, or pushed you. I'm sorry for every time I called you a fag or something else along those lines. I'm at fault. Jonah's a homophobe. Ryders my best friend, yet I still did all that just because you're gay."

I looked at him in disbelief. He did have a different look in his eyes. Not at all disgusted as he looked at me.

"First of all, I'm not gay in the first place. Second, why are you apologizing?" I asked.

"Because...I was wrong and feel really, really bad. I don't want it to be awkward. You don't have to forgive me, or even acknowledge me really. I'll stay out of your hair for now on. Or make it up to you somehow."

That was...good, I guess. So Mattson turned weird, and Marcus turned nice? And Ryder turned protective, and I was...turning...

"It's okay." I said quietly. I can tell he wasn't lying and he really wanted to apologize. "But, Jonah's going to be a handful." I stated. Marcus was his friend too, so why wouldn't he be mad now that he decided to befriend me?

"I don't give a fuck. Ryder's more of my bro than he is, Jason's a jerk and everyone knows it."

"Tell me about it." I muttered.

"So," He breathed. "We cool? I'll try my best to keep him off your back; If you need anything, just ask me, okay? I want to make it up to you."

I smiled a little. "Thanks Marcus. It's okay, really." At least, it will be. It doesn't go away just like that. He knows it too.

He smiled apologetically one more time before walking off. Ryder, finally, made it out of the class and came up to me. "Were you talking to Marcus?"

I shrugged, feeling oddly relieved. "He apologized."

Ryder smiled. "That's great, now we're all good."

I nodded slightly while asking myself, am I finally making friends? I felt a smile creep up to my face but I forced it down. There was no reason to smile Nathan.

"Come on, we have PE together right?"

... "We have PE today?"

"Yeah, it's Friday, remember?"

No. I didn't. I had completely forgot. I nodded slightly and we headed toward the gym. We only have PE maybe once or twice a week, and every Friday. Ryder was in my class, but I've never really noticed anybody other than Jonah.

"I have to get my clothes from my locker, you go ahead." I said with a smile. He nodded and went ahead. I was still getting strange stares. Most people didn't know who I was, so it must be really weird to see Ryder walking with me.

I rushed to my locker and grabbed my clothes, then headed to the locker room to get changed. I was about to push through the door when I realized something.

It was locked.

I tried again. It was manually locked from the inside. There was an explosive laughter behind the door and even though I was alone, I felt my face redden and get a bit angry. Was I purposely locked out?

"Can someone open the door?" I called. Class started soon, and I was never late.

"Yeah right fag, so you can–"

There was a loud crash from the other side and I went still wondering what was going on. The door was yanked open and there was Ryder with a glare plastered on his face. Jonah was behind him, clutching his nose.

"What the fuck!" Jonah shouted. Marcus appeared at his side and hauled him to his feet.

"Come on man, let's go." As they passed, Marcus gave a barely perceptible nod in my direction. The rest of the guys that had been in there retreated out of the locker room in an attempt to avoid Ryder's rage.

"Are you okay?" I asked him when he calmed down.

He laughed bitterly. "Yeah, just mad. He called you that right in front of me."

"He's done it before in front of you, act like you have before. There's no reason to get mad over it." I shrugged past him to one of the locker's in the room and put my bag and stuff in. I glanced at him when I took out the clothes from the kit. He didn't move from where he leaned against the wall.

"Um, do you mind?" I asked.

"Not at all, go on." He smiled slightly and I rolled my eyes. Sure, he saw my scars, but I was overly self-conscious. I grabbed my running clothes and locked myself in a stall to change. When I came out I found him nodding off while still leaning against the wall. I walked up to him and clapped my hands in front of his face. He jumped and muttered something incoherent before he motioned me to hurry along as we made our way to the field.

"Maybe you should hang with Jonah and Marcus during class." I commented before we entered.

"Why?"

"One, he really doesn't like me. Two, he'll think we're friends. Three, he really doesn't like me. Four, wouldn't it be strange if you suddenly started hanging out with some loner? Five, he really doesn't like me. Six, you already stood up for me, you don't need to stick by my side. Seven, did I mention he really doesn't like me?"

He stared at me before laughing. "Okay, my turn. One, I don't care if he likes you. Two, we are friends, or so I thought all on my own. Three is a really stupid reason, because it doesn't matter if he likes you. Four, you are not a loner, you made two friends in the past week," I'm assuming he meant him and Marcus, excluding Mattson, "Five, he's a jerk, you don't want him liking you in the first place. Six, I'll stick by you all day long. Seven, I like you. That's pretty much all that matters."

I like you. I like you. What did he mean by that? As a friend?

"I've managed this entire year, and the years before. Besides you're pretty much attracting the attention of most of the school by staying by me, and it's...weird."

He looked a little disappointed. "Do you not want me by you?"

Did he really want to be by me? I mean, he has so many friends that must be actually fun to hang around, and he's still here arguing with me?

"I already see you after school; don't make me suffer looking at your face all day too." I said sarcastically.

He rolled his eyes and muttered, "I'm hot and I know it. But whatever." before joining the class outside.

It was nice being able to talk normally with someone. I smiled a bit before joining myself. Class was just beginning and the teacher didn't notice us slip to the back. Ryder, as I asked, joined Marcus on the side. Jonah was there too, and Ryder simply apologized–insincerely, might I add–while doing that handshake all guys do to say you're cool.

I stood in the back trying my best to be ignored.

"Okay, three laps around the track then flag-football. Let's go!" Mr. Whatever shouted. Great. The class groaned before following commands and breaking out into steady jogs. I wasn't athletic but I'm not one to walk when we're supposed to be running, and though I'd rather have stayed in the back, it was too hard not to go ahead of the slow guys. Eventually, I passed Ryder, Jonah, Marcus and some of his other friends who were just goofing around. I finished before the rest of the class.

"You should join the track team." The coach commented before reassembling the class and passing out the belts with strips of rubber hanging down.

"And the soccer team while you're at it." Ryder muttered as he passed. I smiled a bit knowing he was annoyed that I was faster than him.

I retrieved a flagged belt and snapped it around my waist and joined the team I had been put with. I may be a good runner, but I still hated PE and all of the sports our teacher makes us do.

We positioned ourselves on the field with me in the far back, hoping I could get by with running around in circles and not being passed to.

They hiked the ball and soon everyone was running around me with full knowledge of what they were doing. Me? I had no idea.

Half way through a guy on my team with the same coloured flags caught my eye. He was surrounded as well as all of our other teammates. I was wide open. So as predicted, he tossed it to me. I caught it without hassle, and coincidentally I was close to the goal. I was prepared to run it in, if someone hadn't run straight into me.

The person had charged from the side and sent both of us knocked to the ground. The wind was choked out of me and he crushed my leg.

Jonah got up and spat, "Can't run now, can you Ms. Strauss?"

"Simmons, what the hell was that? This is flag not tackle!" The teacher shouted from across the field. He was let go with a wave and my breathing slowly returned. He walked away with a new jump in his step.

"You okay?" I looked up at Ryder. Where did he come from?

"Great." He helped me up and I handed him the ball. My leg was sore but nothing seemed to be wrong.

"He's such an ass." I jumped and looked to my other side where Marcus had appeared.

"I'm glad we all agree." Ryder glared at Jonah's back as the game started up again. He threw the ball in a graceful arch to the center. "Just don't catch the ball, and everything should be good, 'kay?"

I shrugged and moved so I was some ways away from the game but not out of bounds. The rest of the period flew by with me trying to avoid the players with the ball, while still making an effort to look like I was playing.

I was exhausted when the class ended. The teacher dismissed us and everyone all but ran to the locker rooms. My legs were sore so I simply walked the remainder of the way. By the time I got there, lunch period had started and everyone should be gone. I checked the doors. Hey, it was open.

Also, it was empty. I could imagine Ryder stuffing his face with food right about now. It made me happy yet a tad bit sad that he was somewhere else, but this is what I wanted. I was too tired to think about eating.

I opened my locker and something fell out. I picked it up. It was a blindfold and a note, reading, 'So you don't spy on us when we change –J'.

I hate him. Why was he pushing this so much? Plus, did it really matter if someone were? It did not! And he definitely shouldn't be giving people a hard time because of it!

I smashed the note up and threw it away along with the blindfold. I don't care. It's not like I've cared before.

I picked off my shirt, glad I didn't sweat too much unlike the other guys.

"I never would have thought you, of all people, would have secrets to hide." My heart rocketed to the sky in shock as I jumped around.

I hadn't heard the door open, but there it was. Open, with Mattson standing in the way.

I scrambled to find my shirt in my locker and soon found it amongst my things. I was about to pull it on if he hadn't strided in and stopped in front of me. I was paralyzed.

"How did...where did you get all of those?" He asked quietly while reaching forward. I stepped back in fright.

"Don't touch me." I whispered.

The silence was eerie as he stared at me with assessing eyes. Before I could react his hand was caressing my cheek. My skin shivered from his cold touch, and the rest of me pretty much fell into a silent trauma. Calm down Nathan. It doesn't matter if he saw your scars. It doesn't matter at all. What matters, is that you hurry up and put that shirt on!

Snapping back to reality I shoved his hand away and pulled the long-sleeve over my head. I moved around him to get to my things and stuffed everything in my backpack.

"Hey," I turned back to him when he spoke. "I won't tell anyone."

I narrowed my eyes at him. He stared back calmly and sincerely before turning around the corner to his locker. I turned slowly before running away down the hall. What did he mean? I thought he turned into a jerk?

Forget everything, I told myself, just don't get involved with him.

I was just on edge and tired, and I need to collect myself.

I decided to skip lunch and find somewhere to sit and relax for the next hour. Yeah, the best way to calm some nerves.

A tree some ways off from the field provided a good shady spot. I slumped against the stump and closed my eyes. I didn't want to think about anything. Sadly, that wasn't the case.

I began thinking about Ryder and Marcus. I can't believe I have friends, and they consider me the same. But I was tired. Was it tiring to have friends? I couldn't afford that. I couldn't afford leaning on others. I just needed to make enough money.

Speaking of which...I felt my whole body sigh in depression as I thought about Mr. Stevens. I wonder if he visited the house while I was gone. What must he have been thinking? He probably didn't expect me to know anybody, and spend time out.

Oh well. As I let myself relax, I thought of one thing. It brought the slightest smile to my lips.

Ryder will be mad I didn't eat lunch.

Chapter ~Fourteen~

•

"So...where are we going to work?" I asked as we left the school. I was heading to work, but staying later when I would normally be tutoring Ryder. I pretty much demanded that we get started on the math project right away. Of course, they protested, but Ryder was the first to give in.

"Not my house." Marcus said. "My parents are working, and they don't trust me home alone, especially with Ryder."

"Hey, it was a minor accident involving the blender and an unmentionable substance."

I resisted asking what the unmentionable substance was. "Oh...okay then. What about your house?" I asked Ryder.

He shook his head. "I have a feeling we'd be interrupted by someone."

"Who?" I asked.

"My slave."

"You mean Mattson?"

"Yeah."

"Ah."

"What about your house?" Marcus asked me. I smiled and scratched the back of my head uneasily. "My parents are on a trip and I'm not allowed to have friends over." I lied easily.

I felt Ryder's eyes on me but ignored it. Marcus nodded and spoke thoughtfully out loud, "The libraries closed, and teachers are gone...hey what about that café place?"

... "You mean the Red Rose?" He nodded. "There's no problem with it. But that was...random."

He shrugged. "I like it there. It's quiet. Plus, then you wouldn't have to meet up with us after your shift right?"

"I guess."

"Okay, then let's go." He began pushing Ryder who yawned sleepily from his previous nap in math.

I felt a little nervous. Were they going to stay while I worked? They'd probably get bored. I had to talk to Kristy before work, I wonder if I'll still be able to.

"I'm going in through the back." I told them as they entered. I ran to the back entrance and through to the back rooms. Kristy was there tying her apron around her neck.

"Hey Kris."

"Hi Nate." She finished the knot with a tug and turned to me. "So, about this morning. What were you going to say, before we were rudely inter-rupted?"

"What?" I asked.

"About Ryder. Did he do anything? Of course he did. What did he do?" She asked excitedly.

"Jeez, nothing! I don't know why you think anything happened. I was sick, he gave me medicine. Ooh, that's definitely worth headline news." I finished sarcastically.

She rolled her eyes and dropped her joking manner. Wait, was it possible for her to act serious? I felt uncomfortable under her stare and squirmed knowing my lie was useless. I bit my lip and looked away. I was giving in. Should I just tell her about what happened? She wouldn't think of me any differently, right?

"Hah! So something did happen! Did he hurt you?"

"No! Why would you think something happened?"

She pouted. "I'm your best friend. You bite your lip when you're thinking about something."

I should probably stop doing that then.

She sat on a stool, crossed her arms, and stared me down. Gosh! Why do I feel so squeamish under her knowing gaze?

Don't give in Nathan!

Yeah right, this is Kristy I'm talking about. I whispered in her ear the one thing that blew my mind above all else that he did. I stepped away a little fearful. Her jaw dropped and her eyes widened to the size of cake dishes. Then she sighed in relief.

"Oh, thank god."

"What?" I asked. I just told her...that...and she's acting completely normal?

"I thought he hurt you. Okay, now that I'm assured he did nothing of the sort," She got up, dusted off her apron, looked me in the eye, and started squealing.

I clamped a hand over her mouth but her eyes continued to sing with joy. Why was she so happy?

I finally let go of her mouth and she continued with her odd noises. "Oh my gosh! That's so cute! He likes you! He likes you! Wait, did you let him? Did you like it?

I suppose it wasn't bad, did he? I didn't really care that it was witha fit, but this guy was Ryder. That's weird right? It didn't feel weird.

"Ah! You're biting your lip! My Nathan is growing up!" She started jumping up and down and I realized, I lost. I shouldn't have told her. She'll act weird now.

"Look, Kristy, I have honestly no idea why you're acting like-"

"He kissed you!" She whisper-shouted. My face felt oddly heated as I looked at my feet. "Nathan, have I ever told you how cute you are? Oh my God! I just can't believe it! I thought he, I don't know, told you his mother prefers you over him or something simple like that, not...Oh my god! You two are going to make the perfect couple-"

"Kris, I don't like him!" She shut up immediately and stared at me with such intensity as before I regretted interrupting her. "What do you mean?" She asked.

"I mean," I felt really bad for some odd reason for saying I didn't like him. I sat down in one of the chairs, and she did the same. As quickly, and quietly as I could, I told her everything. From fainting, to leaving this morning. I finished with, "I-I l...like...him, but I've never liked someone before and I don't know if this is right! I mean, isn't...or... I don't know! He's confusing me! I don't like being confused." I rushed out while shutting my eyes. I would have never told anyone that, or even thought it, hadn't Kristy been the one forcing it out of me.

There was silence and I peeked open. Kristy was smiling at me like the older sister she is. "Nate..."

"What?"

She hugged me. My body didn't tense up, surprisingly. I guess I was getting used to her hugging me. She whispered fondly, "Listen, Nathan, you may not realize it just yet, but when you like someone," I hugged her back. Kristy's touch was reassuring. It really was like hugging a sister. "You feel like that. So in other words,"

She held me out in front of her and her excitement returned. "I'm getting you two together!"

Oh. My god.

What have I done?

-

-

"Would you like anything else?" I asked while tipping my head that contained the usual smile.

The girls in front of me smiled shyly and giggled. "No, but it would be nicer if you would stay." A brunette said.

I laughed like Kristy taught me to do when I didn't understand something, and didn't know what to say in return. "My shift is ending, and I have something to do. Enjoy your meal. Have a good day." I smiled and nodded my head as I walked backward before retreating to the back room.

This was an extremely awkward shift. I swear, Marcus and Ryder were staring at me the entire time. Creepers. Once I saw Marcus laughing and Ryder crossing his arms, refusing to look anywhere but the table. I wonder what happened.

I changed out of uniform and grabbed my bag. Kristy will still be working, and she said she will take our booth. I don't know why, and I desperately hoped she wasn't planning anything.

I approached the table. Even if Ryder's smile seemed a little forced, it almost made me stop walking and made my throat feel dry. Why? I shook my head clear of the delusions and slid in next to Marcus, feeling that if I got close to him, I'd have a problem speaking.

"Enjoy watching me work?" I asked casually, expecting a sarcastic remark or something.

Ryder shrugged and looked away to the side with his arms crossed over his chest. Why was he grumpy?

"What's wrong?" I asked and looked up at him worriedly. Maybe he wasn't feeling well.

His eyes flickered to me and his mouth parted a bit. He faced me a little more and continued to open and close his mouth, with nothing coming out. I frowned and looked up at him closely. Nothing seemed wrong. Was it me? I must have done something.

"Erm, should we order?" Marcus suggested. I nodded slowly and looked at him to see if he noticed Ryder's behavior. He seemed fine, in fact he was smiling and just hid a laugh with a cough.

Ryder seemingly snapped out of his reverie and shook his head fiercely. Okay...

"Hey guys, Nate, what do you guys want?" Wow, she wasn't even bothering with the usual introductions a host would start with.

"Water." I told her awkwardly. Of course it would be awkward, to have your friend serving you.

She frowned a little and poked my stomach. "Please don't tell me you eat water for breakfast, lunch, and dinner."

"Yes I only drink water for every meal because it's just so delicious." I responded.

"Sarcasm is not appreciated, mister. What about you two?" Ryder ordered something and when Marcus didn't respond she looked at him over her notepad. I looked at him as well. He was just staring at Kristy. I looked back up at the said girl to find her cheeks a tipsy red as she stared back.

"Hello? You two okay?" I asked. Ryder coughed in his hand and I found him hiding a smile.

"Uh, sorry. I'll have a coke and surprise me with an appetizer." She nodded, writing it in her notes and rushed back through the kitchen. Hm, usually she would talk more. Oh well.

"So about the project-"

"Is Kristy your girlfriend?" Marcus asked.

I spluttered, "W-what? No!"

"Really?" I looked at Ryder who had spoken. What was that look he was giving me?

"No. We're close friends." He looked down at the saltshaker he played with.

Marcus nodded and looked back at his hands. I shook my head at their weird behavior and pulled the papers for the project from my bag. We began discussing what we needed for the project but the two kept getting distracted by the cakes on the menu.

Minutes later Kristy came back with our meals. I just remembered I skipped lunch and I was hungry, but ignored it and sipped from my water. The two began digging in.

"Ryder, I swear, you never grew out of eating sweets." Marcus laughed. Ryder stuffed more of the desert in his mouth. It was the cake I made, I realized.

"Is it good?" I asked. I've always wondered if people actually think it's good.

"Delicious."

I smiled a little. "Thanks."

He cleared his throat and we got back to looking at the project details. We were interrupted when two girls, the last customers I had served, got up from their table and stopped at our booth on the way out. "Bye Nathan." They said together with grins.

"Uh, bye." I said a little awkwardly. Weird. "So about this equation-"

"Do you know them?" Why was I being interrupted so much today?

"No." I said with a straight face, a little annoyed at Ryder for asking something so ridiculously obvious.

"Could've fooled me, you know you're awfully friendly with your customers."

"Have you ever worked as a waiter?" I said slowly, not really sure what he was getting at.

He looked thoroughly irritated. To be honest, regardless of whatever his problem was, I was surprised with how well he was handling it compared to before.

"Hey there's this thing in the back I need help lifting, can one of you help me?" Kristy appeared out of nowhere, making me jump. I was about to get up but Marcus beat me to it.

"I'll help you, you two stay here and figure yourselves out." The two disappeared behind the kitchen.

.:~* MARCUS*~:. (HE'S IMPORTANT, HE NEEDS A POV!)

I have never, and I mean never, seen Ryder this jealous. And honestly, I've never seen anyone as dense as Nathan. The poor kid is confused. God, they would be perfect for eachother.

I watched Ryder carefully as he watched Nathan as he worked. What a stalker. There was giggling to our side as Nathan conversed with two girls.

I laughed when I saw Ryder glare fiercely away and cross his arms. Nathan disappeared to the back.

"Gosh dude, he's just doing his job. Did you see his face? He has no idea they were flirting with him."

"Whatever."

Minutes later he came out and Ryder was still acting like shit. God, get over it!

But then Nathan looked up at him like my dog when begging for food with worry filling his eyes, and I tried so hard not to laugh when Ryder got lost while looking at him.

Please don't tell me someone was getting a little too happy.

"Hey guys, Nate, what do you want?"

I wanted to laugh again because of how Ryder watched with a glare at how easily Nathan talked with our waitress. I decided to look up at the second person to make Ryder jealous, and wouldn't you know it? It's the hottest girl alive.

Beautiful, I meant. Yes, beautiful. She had a long blond braid, with a fringe that perfectly outlined her heart-shaped face. Her green eyes almost entranced me like Nathan had done to Ryder.

I was drawn to this girl.

The worst part?

She wasn't even trying.

She looked at me suddenly, and I completely forgot we were in the presence of others. Her green eyes were so...at lost for better words, green.

I snapped out of it and ordered. I accidently burst out asking Nathan if she was his girlfriend, and I tried to convince myself it was for Ryder's sake, since he seemed interested in his answer. He was jealous, so of course he was interested.

Then the second best thing happened that afternoon. She came back.

"...can one of you help me?" I jumped up at the occasion, seeing it as a chance to leave Ryder and Nathan together. Instead of thinking for myself like a normal guy would, and go so I can flirt with her, I had to focus on my other agenda.

I had to help Ryder out. And apparently, this was Nathan's best friend.

We didn't even go to the back, instead I was pulled below the counter. She peeked carefully over the counter at the booth I was previously in.

"Uh, what are we doing?" I asked.

"Okay, here's the deal, you're Ryder's best friend right?" I nodded slowly. "I know I'm extremely good at reading people. And I know that Ryder's gay, or bi or whatever. The point is we need to get those two, together."

...

She doesn't waste any time, does she?

"You know, I was about to say the same exact thing." I shook my head in disbelief. She looked at me, "Really?" She even sounded cute...

I mean, "Yup. I guess you know that Ryder has this thing for him, then?"

"I guess you know Ryder kissed him already, then?"

My jaw dropped. "No way..." What the hell man? Couldn't he fill me in on why he was absent for those few days?

She squealed this adorable sound and nodded. "I can't believe it either. But here's the thing, Nathan is an idiot."

"Some best friend you are." I laughed.

She shrugged. "It's true. He's dense, and confused. He doesn't know when people flirt, or even when he likes someone, which by the way, happens to be Ryder."

"Really? That's...wow, my job just got easier. So what's the deal? Are we going to get them together?" Hah, why was I so excited about this? Maybe because I always knew Nathan was a good kid. I felt a nauseous wave of guilt, thinking back to what I've done to him before. I hate that. I peeked over the counter and felt my eyes narrow.

Ryder was ignoring him.

What the fuck?! Was he seriously that jealous over something so small?

Nathan's hands were tight in his lap and his face looked worried. I can tell he was annoyed and hurt, but he was extremely good at hiding it. Good thing I was just as good as... "What's your name?"

"Kirsty."

Just as good as Kristy at observing things. Suddenly she grabbed the front of my shirt and forced me against the counter. My breathing hitched as she stared at me straight in the eyes.

"Look. Nathan has gone through a lot of fucking shit. He works every freaking day, as much as he can. He's been hurt more times than he can count, and not just by you and your friend, Jonah was it? Yeah I'm a stalker. I can tell he forgave you, so, so am I. I know Ryder is okay, but if this really is a stupid joke, then I suggest you make him stop it right now. I will not see Nathan hurt."

I stared at her stunning courage. I know. I won't hurt Nathan anymore. I can't hurt him. I realize that now. And I won't let Ryder mess this up. I owe them. "It's not a joke. I won't hurt him again, I just can't do that. I swear on my life, if Ryder fucks up, I'll kill him."

She smiled with so much happiness, I almost fainted. "Thanks. But, here's a tip: don't swear around Nate. Or touch him."

I frowned. "Why?"

She smiled sadly. "Not my place to say."

I nodded. "I get it. I wont ask. So, how should we push things along?" She got the hint at the change of subject and beamed.

"Movies."

Chapter ~Fifteen~

:~* NATHAN *~:.

●

I think I did something wrong. Ryder seemed mad. After Marcus came back, from doing whatever Kristy needed his help with, Ryder did his best to control his speech and only talk about the project.

Marcus lived by Ryder, we were about to part ways and I turned to say bye, when Ryder walked ahead.

No bye? Thanks.

"Don't worry about him, his time of the month. Hey, we're going to the movies tomorrow since it's Saturday. You're coming right?"

"Sorry, busy." I answered immediately. Actually. I needed to go around looking for temporary jobs. The cafe was closed tomorrow.

"Doing what?"

"Um, work."

He smiled mischievously. "Where?"

"The cafe." I lied easily.

"You're a good liar. That's not a good thing. I know it's closed, that's why Kristy is coming. You're coming too, don't try to get out of it. I'm paying so don't worry. See you tomorrow then. Bye."

"Wai-"

"Bye!" He shouted again and ran off to catch up with Ryder.

But I don't want to waste my time at the...movies? I've never gone to the movies. Do people there have good pay?

-

-

"Nathan, I need to buy you new clothes, those are old." Kristy eyed my jeans and T-shirt. What was she talking about? They were still big on me!

"Whatever, let's get this over with." I grumbled. I didn't want to be here.

I didn't even know this town had a movie cinema. Apparently this was where people went on the weekends, either to the movies or arcade, then the food court.

Ryder and Marcus came together whereas Kristy came by and we walked together. She really did know where I lived, which is really disturbing.

I felt weird being surrounded by so much people. I was only wearing a long sleeve. I planned on wearing a huge sweater but Kristy made me take it off before we left, since it was hot.

I tugged on my sleeves and looked at the ground. Why did Marcus bring us to the movies? And why was Kristy here? They just met yesterday!

"Hey!" Marcus waved as they approached. I found myself looking at Ryder, who dressed casually but still managed to look...I shook my head fiercely. No. Bad Nathan.

Was he feeling better? I wonder why he was mad yesterday. He looks better, but he didn't acknowledge us yet. Maybe he didn't want to be here as much as I. I wouldn't have minded if we had tutoring today. At least we'd be at the house and comfortable.

"So, what were we going to see?" I asked.

"Chic-flick." Marcus responded.

Ryder made a disgusted face, "What? Seriously? Why am I here then?"

He began walking away but Marcus grabbed his collar and hauled him back. "Come on, Kristy wants to see it."

Ryder looked at her. "Why are you here?"

She pouted. "I'm Nathan's best friend. I go where I want."

Ryder shook his head. "I'm not sitting through an hour of watching a messed up couple getting more messed up before one of them dies, then the best friend steals the girl."

"Fine." Marcus said, raising his hands in defense. "I'll go with Kristy. Nathan, you want to come?"

"I'm going home." I dead-panned. I began walking away but Kristy grabbed my arm that I yanked away frantically.

"Sorry, wrong arm." She said apologetically, I shrugged. "Don't leave! Hey, you and Ryder can go to another movie and we'll all meet at the arcade, okay? Just stick together and we'll go play some games later."

"Why? I have to-" I stopped and glanced at Marcus. Hah, he was the only one that didn't know. Finally, someone that didn't know my life story. "Never mind."

"Great. Here, I'll still pay for your tickets." Marcus handed Ryder a twenty but he shoved it back.

"I have my own money."

He shrugged and took Kristy's hand. "Kay, we'll see you guys later. Bye!"

Why didn't they seem the least bit bothered that we weren't going with them? They ran off eagerly around the corner. Wait, the ticket booth was the other way. Did they already get their tickets, knowing we wouldn't want to watch a chick-flick? Oh my god, what were they planning?

"Let's go." Ryder seemed a little void of emotion, but he seemed relaxed and not annoyed like yesterday.

We got to the booth and I was about to pull out a ten for my ticket, but he put down a twenty and ordered for an action thing.

"I could've paid for it." I said.

"No, you couldn't have." He said in a matter-of-fact voice. He sighed, raised his hand and slapped himself on the cheek. I jumped. "Sorry, I didn't mean it like that. I wanted to pay."

I kept my gaze on my hands and the conversation kind of stopped there as we entered the movie. We were early, and the movie from before had just ended and people were leaving. Ryder led the way inside but I was caught in the wave. A couple people bumped into me and I decided to stick to the wall until the wave passed.

A hand grabbed my right wrist and I was pulled through the doorway. I looked up at Ryder.

"Thanks." He helped me and managed to remember that my left side was off-limits.

I swear I saw a hint of a smile but he was already pulling to the middle row where the best seats were. We sat down and on cue the lights dimmed as the rest of the people entered. It was cold with the air-con in here and...

It was dark. But the large screen in front shot shadows everywhere. After the endless credits, the sound got considerably louder and the movie began.

There was a lot of action, and killing, and destroying. What were we watching? There was the occasional romance between the main guy and the girl. Near the end things started to get unexpectedly...intense. I averted my eyes and squirmed in my seat, holding my arms close.

I shut my eyes and did my best to block out the sounds of their, er, moment. I felt extremely out of place. It just felt really, really wrong to be seeing someone do this willingly when I was...I shook my head.

Suddenly the cold air wasn't licking my face. Instead I opened my eyes to see nothing but black. I was warm, and this clean smell wafted up my nose. I felt an arm go around my shoulders and I was held awkwardly across the armrest.

"I swear the sign said this was PG." Ryder muttered. I looked at what covered me. It was his black jacket.

"It's fine." I said while feeling thankful he couldn't see how embarrassed I was.

He scoffed and didn't let go the rest of the movie, even after the scene ended. Warmth from his side seeped through my clothing. It wasn't that bad. At least no one could see us. Or my ridiculous expression.

The movie ended with the credits rolling by so fast, there didn't seem a point in putting it in.

"Let's go to the arcade." He suggested.

"Um, okay." We got up and I noticed he didn't take back his jacket. In the crowded place, I felt a lot more secure with it. We entered the colorful arcade.

"Have you ever played these games before?" He asked smiling. Bipolar person. I guess he was feeling fine now.

"No. How?" I asked. He smirked and put my hands on the buttons of the arcade game. It was a skateboarding thing.

"Now press that button," He pointed across the wide panel, "Over there."

"Which one?"

He went behind me and maneuvered my hands. I watched the screen like it was witchcraft. His body warmth spread through the jacket and I was glad I was faced away so he didn't see my face. He was getting really close; it only made me feel warmer. I thought we were in public?

"You won." He said in my ear. A tingle shot down my spine and I jumped slightly.

"Yay." I stepped away from the machine and smiled while looking anywhere but his face.

He started laughing at my uneasiness. "Hey Nathan?"

"Yeah?"

"You didn't flinch when I touched you."

"I didn't?" I asked. I looked at my hands. He's right. I hadn't flinched. In fact, I kind of missed the warmth he gave. "Oh, um, yeah. I mean-"

"I guess you're getting used to me." He laughed again before muttering, "Gosh, where are those two?"

Ryder tapped his foot and crossed his arms. He was adorable when impatient. The jacket was big, so the sleeves hung past my hands. I hid my laugh behind it. I couldn't help it, he was really cute. And Kristy said I looked like a puppy when I pouted.

He looked at me with wide eyes. "What?" I asked still smiling.

"N-nothing." He stammered. His cheeks flushed a deep red. "I'm going to get some drinks. Wait here for the other two."

He rushed back inside the arcade where there was a concession bar. He was walking strangely.

I leaned against the wall and inhaled deeply. I was thinking differently today. I just want to be near him. Was it wrong? Because as far as I knew it was true. Even his scent, I'll admit in my mind, smelled really nice.

"Since when were faggots allowed here?" I opened my eyes and glared at Jonah. I've never seen him outside of school, and I'd rather it have stayed that way.

"Isn't that Ryder's jacket?" I looked at his friends. They hadn't even noticed me until Jonah stopped them. I think they were the rest of the guys on the soccer team.

Jonah stared at the jacket. "Is Ryder here?" He asked.

I wasn't sure what to say. Yes? He'd probably explode. No? I'd be lying, he would know it, and he would still explode.

Jonah stepped up to my face. His friends shuffled uneasily behind him, knowing where this would lead. One of them grabbed his arm but he shoved them off. "What are you doing, faggot? Trying to get in his pants? Take his money?"

"W-what?" I said in disbelief. "No-"

"Then what?" He shoved me and I stumbled back. "Huh? Trying to turn everyone into a fag like you?"

"I'm not-"

He shoved me hard making me unable to finish that sentence.

"You know, he's been hanging around you a lot. What, are you black mailing him or something? I'm getting tired of Ryder thinking you're worth shit. You're not. You're a worthless fag, so stay out of our lives." He yelled.

"I'm not a-" I shouted, then finished my sentence quickly. "–a fag. I'm not a fag. So stop calling me that! What's your problem?"

Jonah wasn't used to me shouting back, and he obviously didn't like it. He ripped the cover off his drink and before I knew it, the soda was dripping down my face and through my clothes. My hair became matted to my forehead and neck.

I shut my eyes before the stinging of the drink and sputtered and shook my head to get rid of the droplets. Jonah laughed hysterically.

I looked around. A lot of the people had stopped what they were doing and now stared at the little circle. Some started giggling and laughing at my state.

"Come on Ms. Strauss, aren't you going to ask what I'll be having today? Aren't you going to smile like the good fag you are? Come on, smile! That's all you did the other day when you got wet on the floor. Did you have a hard time getting up?"

More of the teens started laughing. I shook my head. That's all I could do.

"Come on dude, stop it." One of his friends placed a hand on his shoulder again. Jonah glared at him. "He's a fag, and fucking turning Ryder into one too! Go on, have some fun."

Jonah nodded at the drink they all carried. I was rooted to the spot, afraid to say anything, afraid to run. I was embarrassed. All these people were laughing. With Jonah. At me.

"Do it!" Jonah shouted at his friends. "Or else you know what's going to happen." They were at a loss at what to do. I stared at the nearest guy. He didn't look me in the eye as he uncapped his drink and in a moment I was drenched again. His friends followed and the process repeated. Again. Again. And again. In less than a minute I was soaked with soda and juice. I looked at the sleeves of Ryders jacket which also got soaked and felt ashamed.

"Sticky much?" Jonah sneered. The guys behind him didn't laugh but didn't look at me either.

I shook my head and stared at the ground. "What did I do? What did I ever do to you?"

He glared with that chilling grin that reassured me he was still mad. "Fag's don't need to do anything. You fucking deserve this."

"Deserve this?" I whispered in disbelief.

I began shivering, partly from the icy drinks. I felt a gaze that penetrated through all the others. Where was he? I looked to the side. Ryder stood there stock still with wide eyes and jaw dropped. He just stared, trying to understand what was going on.

I looked back at Jonah, and his friends, then the people around me. Everyone blended into one. I was weak. Pathetic. With a last look at Ryder, I did the only thing I could.

I ran.

Chapter ~Sixteen~

- -

:~* NATHAN *~:.

•

I wasn't crying. No. Why would I cry? I'm used to it. Crying doesn't do anything. It shows you're even more weak than people thought you were. So I held it back and bit my tongue. I forcibly blinked and pushed my legs harder through the cinema. I needed somewhere to sit and calm down where people wont stare. I just wanted to be alone for a moment, like how things used to be before I met Ryder.

Ryder.

I bit my tongue harder.

I found a bathroom near the entrance. It was empty so I locked myself in one of the stalls. I leaned against the door and slid down to a sitting position. I stayed absolutely still and breathed deeply.

There was a squeak as the bathroom door opened. If that was Jonah, how the heck am I going to get out of here? Alive?

But the voice was too familiar to be his. "Nathan?" Ryder's voice broke my much-needed silence.

I breathed deeply. I saw his shoes stop in front of the stall. "Nate! I'm sorry. I dealt with them. Are you okay? Did he hurt you? I swear if he-"

"I'm fine." I said. I really was. I wasn't hurt, or scared. Just really tired of his annoying antics. I got up and brushed myself off, opening the door.

I was tackled further into the stall. "What are you-?" I could barely breathe. Was he hugging me? "Ryder, you're kind of killing me."

"Sorry." He held me at arm's length and I took in a big breath of air and stared back in surprise.

"Ryder," I said slowly, "Please don't tell me you did anything stupid, to any of your friends or Jonah."

"I was too shocked, so I could only manage one punch." He said. I sighed in relief. If he did any more, Jonah would harass me the rest of my life. "Your friend Kristy beat me to it."

"What!" Oh Kristy, what have you done?

"Yeah, I was kind of surprised. Marcus had to pull her off of them. I swear, I had never met a girl with enough balls to kick someone in the balls." He chuckled at one of his thoughts. "Man, he will definitely be having some trouble walking for a while..."

Oh god. I groaned. I stared at my feet shuffling on the ground. "Ryder, I- I don't know if you heard anything. B-but I'm not trying to do anything to you. I'm sorry. I'm not after your money; I'm not doing any of those things he said. I'm not like that. Pleas-"

He lifted my chin so I stared straight in his grey eyes. Uh...what were we talking about...? "What are you saying? He's the ass. I know for a fact that none of what he said was true. I know, better than anyone else. That includes Kristy. You don't need to convince me of anything."

My heart. Something was wrong with my heart. It was beating really fast. I bit my lip, and I knew he hadn't expected me to hug him fiercely back. He wrapped his arms around me and rested his chin on my head.

"It's about time." We jumped apart. When did Marcus get there? And... Kristy?

"Kristy, what are you doing in the men's bathroom?" I hissed.

"My best friend could be getting hypothermia from soda and all you care about is me being in the wrong bathroom? Well too bad, 'caus I love you too much to care." She hugged me fiercely too. It didn't feel the same as when Ryder did it, and I felt ashamed thinking so. "Are you okay? You don't need to worry. I taught that Jonah a lesson in Kung Fu, and let me tell you, he sucks-"

"Oh my god Kristy." I groaned and hung my head.

"Shut up, as if I'm going to sit around and allow people to mess with my Natey."

"I told you to stop calling me that when we were thirteen."

"Can I call you that?" Ryder perked up.

"No!" I saw Marcus open his mouth and I glared. "You too!" He shut it and nodded. "Um, can we go now?" I asked. They all nodded and we headed out the door.

Marcus and Kristy walked in front. They got along really well, and it made me wonder what they were whispering about. "Sorry about your jacket." I said to Ryder.

"No problem. Want me to take it for you?"

"No." I said, and realized it might have been said a little too quickly. I blushed and looked away. I still wanted to wear it. "I mean, I'll wash it and give it to you on Monday. If that's okay."

"No." He shook his head firmly. Wha-? "You'll give it back tomorrow."

"I'm not going to see you tomorrow. No tutoring, and I'm working–"

"Work?" He made a funny face. "Who said I was going to let you work on a weekend like you don't have a life?"

"Um, if you haven't noticed, I dont have a life." I deadpanned. He laughed and shook his head.

"I'm giving you one." He put an arm around my shoulders. I shivered. It felt nice. Like friends, I figured. Friends do that all the time.

"I already rested today, I need to make at least forty an hour tomorrow to make up for today."

He stopped walking and faced me with both hands on my shoulders. "I have it all planned. And I'm not really giving you a choice." He took a big breath and looked away. "So...I'll pick you up tomorrow, at ten?"

Don't say yes...don't say okay... He looked me in the eye and I heard myself whisper, "Fine."

His smile lit up my entire vision and before I could take a breath Kristy nudged her way into our conversation. "Yay! Natey's going on a date!" She jumped up and down.

"N-no I'm not!" I felt my face heat up.

Ryder's face had a pink shade but he turned to me and spoke first. "I mean technically speaking..."

"What? But-"

Marcus interrupted and took Kristy's hand and asked, "Well, we know what we're doing, right?"

She turned pink but said, "right. Let's get scheming, young man."

"Young man? I'm older than you." Kristy burst laughing and pulled him away. "Come on Ryder, we gotta plan."

"They're getting along well." He said, letting them run ahead.

"I wonder what happened during their movie." We glanced at each other and I couldn't help but laugh.

To think it was so easy to laugh sometimes. It was surprising. Ryder seemed to think the same thing and his grin grew wider. "Okay, I'll see you tomorrow then?"

"Well-"

"Great."

He stared at me for a moment longer before reaching out and ruffling my hair. He tapped me on the cheek once with his finger, then ran off to catch up with Marcus.

I need to see a doctor about my heart.

Chapter ~Seventeen~

•

I loved it when he smiled for real, and that means when he's not faking it like at the café. And when he laughs...ugh, I get happy. If you know what I mean. He started giggling and god, it was so cute I had to walk away just to calm myself.

Then the freaking bitch came. What the hell was wrong with Jonah? What did Nate do? After getting home I called the whole team and sorted things out with them. They were under pressure because Jonah could have them kicked from the team or be sit out. I need to figure something out about that.

Whatever. That didn't matter right now. What mattered was that he opened his door for me and was ready to go, wearing worn out jeans and the usual long-sleeve.

My gaze trailed down his jaw line to his lips. Soft. I can't kiss him. I should wait until he's figured out his feelings. But I could just imagine pressing his lips with my own....

Snap out of it, Ryder.

"How did you find my house?" He asked with a tilt of his head.

"Kristy texted me. What I want to know is how she got my number."

"That girl is crazy." He sighed. "Look, I really have to work today, and–"

"Kristy told Mrs. Clair you're taking the day off." I ratted.

His jaw dropped. "That girl needs her own life. Well...sometimes the drug store downtown let's me work under the table-"

"No!" I interrupted. "You are not working!"

"I need–"

"The money, I know." I plucked two twenties from my pocket and shoved it in his hand. "What's this?" He asked like I was an idiot.

"Money. And that's the before-payment. Since you are obviously against having fun, I guess the only choice is to pay you to hang out. I'll give you the rest after, if you have fun on our date."

He was shaking his head wildly. "No! That's ridiculous. Have you lost your mind? I can't just take someone's money without working for it–"

"I thought you needed the money, and you are working for it, by hanging out. "

He looked me straight in the eye. "I'm not the kind of person to take money like this."

I smiled a little. He was so serious. "I know. Think of this as tutoring, or as an advancement, or like my mom hired you to be my friend. I factored in everything for this date, so you don't have to worry.

His eyes widened and his face flushed deeply. "It's not a... date."

"Right right. You'll be working. It's work. Let's go."

Being the stronger one, I led him gently toward my mom's car. I pushed him into the passenger seat and buckled him in before rushing to my side and driving off before he could get out.

"This is considered kidnapping."

"It's only kidnapping when it's against your will."

"This is against my will. I'm pretty sure I didn't willingly get in your car."

"Yeesh, you make me sound like a dangerous person. Come on, you know you'd rather hang out with me than work." I smiled at him in the mirror. He bit his lip. Haha, I knew that gesture, he was overthinking and knew it was true.

"Where are we going?" He asked with a sigh.

"Somewhere cold, so you can wear the jacket." I inclined my head to my sweater in his arms. I swear I saw him bite his lip again but it was gone before I could see it. He shrugged. I was doing my best to focus on the road, but I could feel each time he glanced at me.

"Where are we going exactly?" He looked at our surroundings as we speeded away from town.

"Almost there." A building came up on our right. It was large with a small parking lot surrounding it. I parked close to the entrance and ran around the car to open the door for him. He looked at me strangely but I only smiled.

This was, after all, a date.

I pulled him to the entrance and paid the thirty-dollar entry for both of us. Mom pitched in and gave three hundred for this evening. I would get a restraining order against Kristy if she somehow got my mom's number and told her about today.

"Why are we at a skating rink?" He asked. I got skates for both of us and sat him on one of the benches so I could begin tying my laces.

"My mom used to bring me here when I was little. I'm assuming you don't know how to skate, but it'll be fun." And you'll have to lean on me.

I finished tying my second skate and found him struggling to make it tight enough. I grinned and took his skate and put it in my lap to tie. I just love seeing him react and feel overly conscious about our positions.

"Come on." I took his hand to guide him to the rink. He must have never skated before; he was wobbling like it was his first steps. I hope he doesn't get hurt.

"Ready?" I asked.

"Wait, I don't think–"

"Let's go." I pulled him out onto the ice. He yelped and grasped onto my arm.

Well, if you insist.

"It's okay, just move your feet like this." I took a couple strides. He stared at the ice before taking small little steps. I laughed. "Come on."

It took a while before he finally decided he wouldn't fall anytime soon. I wouldn't let that happen. Soon he started laughing at me as I showed off skating backwards and swiveling. We took a break by the wall and played with the shaved ice.

"Wow." He breathed. "She's good."

I followed his gaze to the center of the rink where a girl in one of those figure outfits was practicing her jumps and spins. She landed without hesitation, and I felt the need to jab, "almost as good as your run in with the wall earlier." He rolled his eyes.

We watched as she skated in a graceful circle and shifted her weight so naturally. She slowed down to catch her breath and met our eyes. Great, we probably look like stalkers. She smiled and skated over.

"Hi." She breathed, still catching her breath.

"Hey." I said. Nathan smiled politely. He really didn't know how to talk to people other than at the café, did he?

"Like my routine?" She laughed.

"Yeah, you're awesome."

"Thanks." She chewed on her lip and glanced at me and I realized she was flirting. She was attractive, I supposed. She touched my arm and commented, "You know, I saw you earlier, you'd be really good at this."

"You think?" I laughed, pulling my arm away to scratch my head. "I'd probably fall on my face if I even tried to do what you did."

"I could teach you." She tilted her head slightly. Ah, she was trying so hard. I get it, you're attractive, but you must be able to tell I'm being defensive. She must think I'm challenging her, and I smiled knowing she'd be surprised when her efforts are fruitless.

"That'd be interesting but–"

I was about to continue the game then I realized Nathan was staring at the girl and me.

Shit. He probably didn't understand what was happening either. Does it look like I'm flirting? He looked down at his skates and I swear he looked annoyed but covered it up quickly. I can never tell with him, but right now

I knew he was bothered. He shuffled backwards and I realized I shouldn't drag this on.

"-but I'd have to pass on that offer." I smiled sweetly at her and stopped Nathan from going away. I pulled him to my side and stated very clearly, "I'm on a date."

She looked at Nathan and back at me as she realized what I meant. She blushed madly but made a face before clicking her tongue and looking at Nate like he was nothing. "Too bad. I'd have been much more fun." She winked and I rolled my eyes.

"Doubt that." Before I could back down, I leaned down and kissed his forehead.

His skin was cold against my lips, and I waited there, wondering if I could manage to kiss down to his lips. I wonder if he would let me.

"Ugh!" The girl skid away. I wasn't paying attention any more.

I kissed him. Just a little. His eyes were so large and innocent. He seemed to have already forgotten the girl. I leaned in again and kissed to the side of his eye. Nate, if you're going to stop me, stop me now.

"You...just...why..." He breathed. My smile grew a little bigger and I rested my forehead against his.

"Sorry. That girl was annoying me, and I couldn't resist anymore." I let my lips brush his nose and he got even more flustered, "You're not scared." I whispered. He trembles when he's touched, but so far, none of that has happened today.

"What...um, what does this mean? Do you–"

He stopped himself, pursing his lips together. He seemed confused.

"Because I like you." I said, matter of factly. Didn't I tell him this before? Wasn't it obvious?

He blinked. "Like, as in..."

"As in I like you and want to date you. Didn't I tell you before in the locker room? I've even kissed you before."

He looked so confused, but his body seemed to relax as if this has been bothering him for a long time and he finally understood. He closed his eyes and took a deep breath.

"Oh." He said. He smiled. It was small, but it wasn't fake, or polite. Just a true smile only he could make. "Oh, I...I see."

It was beautiful.

I tapped his cheek and he opened his eyes.

"I'm going to kiss you."

When I leaned down and our cold lips touched, he didn't pull away. He was breathing irregularly through his nose like he didn't know how, and I could feel myself smiling against his lips. My fingers found themselves in his hair and I brushed it back.

When I pulled away, his hand instinctively covered his red face. I wouldn't have it. I pinched his cheeks and pulled it back to make him smile. He cocked an eyebrow and I laughed.

"I want to see your smile." I whined. He flicked my hands away with one hand, the other still touching his mouth.

"Come on?" I begged. I sounded like a child. His mouth twitched. "Please? If you do, I'll make Marcus and Kristy go out."

He erupted in laughter and there it was again, his beautiful smile.

Chapter ~Eighteen~

:~* NATHAN*~:.

•

He kissed me.

Ryder kissed me.

I didn't stop it. I didn't hate it. I might even go as far to say I may have liked it. It just felt right. Ever since the first time he kissed me in his room, I realized I've been pushing this aside but today he made me face it.

I realized, that for the first time, I decided to forget my messed up life and forget everything that was confusing me, and look at the present. Look at Ryder. For the first time, I felt like truly smiling and laughing.

Why was I smiling?! I was smiling so easily, it seemed impossible. I began laughing and I couldn't stop. Ryder joined as well but it only made me laugh more.

"I'm sorry." I gasped. "I never...I don't...oh my god." I giggled and looked away, covering my face with my cold hands.

"Blame me for making you happy." I could hear the smile in his voice as he pulled my hands away from my face. I felt my face growing insanely red, and it was pretty useless trying to convince myself it was from the cold.

"Let's skate." He pulled me along again, and I think I did a little better. I was able to keep up with his long strides.

I felt like a kid again, learning to skate. If that was his intention, it was really sweet.

I found that time actually does go by fast when you're having fun, because hours later we were leaving the ice on wobbly legs.

"Hungry?" He asked with a huge smile on his face. I laughed and shrugged, checking my watch. "It's already five, I think I should go home. School tomorrow."

He thought for a moment before shaking his head. "I think you can allow me the pleasure of one more hour. Let's go."

He helped me take off the skates. It felt so weird walking normally. We hopped in the car and I watched curiously as we drove a few minutes to a nice restaurant. It was big, with two floors and low lights that gave it a warm feel. He tugged me out of the car and through the doors.

It smelled amazing. He said, "I know it's different than the Red Rose, but I have connections. You'll love the food. I come here all the time." All the time? Well, he is rich, and this place seemed really fancy.

"Reservation for Kenning?" He told the waitress, an older woman in her twenties. She rolled her eyes. "Ryder, we know who you are. Come on."

I glanced at him curiously but didn't ask anything until we were seated in the back of the restaurant.

Instead of introducing herself as our waitress, she left right away to be replaced by a man in his twenties.

"Hello, boys, what will you be having this fine evening?" He asked with a larger than necessary smile.

Ryder groaned. "I told you not to bus our table tonight!" He whined.

"Aw, come on, I had to see who my little bro's been crushing on!" He gave Ryder a side hug and ruffled his hair. Ryder made a 'tch' sound and pouted. He turned to me and grabbed my hand across the table. It felt different now than when he'd touch me before.

"Hello, my name's Steff, Ryder's older, hotter, more publicly established, smarter, college graduate, did I mention hotter? loved by all woman, and men, handsome–"

"The douche bag's my brother." Ryder interrupted with irritation.

"I'm Nat–"

"Nathan, I've been informed." He winked at his brother who 'huff'ed and looked away. Now that I think about it, they did look alike ...with a matching ego. "I'm the owner of this place."

"It's really nice." I said and looked around longingly. I wonder what the kitchen looked like.

"The food's even better. The usual, Ryder?" He nodded and Steff was gone and back in moments with the drinks. He waited at the end of the table with a large smile as we lapped into awkward silence. Ryder groaned and hit his head repeatedly before shouting, "Leave! Now!" Steff winked again and moved on to the next booth.

Ryder sighed in annoyance and I laughed. "Awesome brother you have there."

"Love him, but am so glad he moved out." He smiled.

"I think it's cool to have someone like him around." I thought out loud. He shrugged.

"You don't need someone like him. You have me. Nathan?"

I blinked at him and took a sip of my drink. "Yeah Ryder?"

He took a deep breath. "I figured I should talk this over clearly this time, so you don't get confused or push this aside. Will you be my boyfriend?"

.:~* RYDER *~:.

He spit out his drink. I'm taking that as a good sign. I smiled a little and watched as his face turned beetroot red.

"Wh-what?" He stuttered.

"You. Me. Boyfriend-boyfriend." He wiped his mouth and bit his lip. Oh god.

"Ryder..." He whispered and looked away. "I-I can't. I...I'm sorry. Work, debt... I just can't. I'm kind of... messed up–"

"Don't say that." I muttered and scooted my chair so I was sitting right next to him. I lifted his chin so he could look at me. "You are the most amazing, beautiful, amazing...did I mention amazing? You're my Natey."

He wrinkled his nose and said, "Ew, don't call me that."

"Which part? Natey or my Natey?"

He blushed and his eyes were glossy. But nothing came out, thankfully. I would have cried along with him if he had.

"Just Natey." His face was the reddest I'd ever seen and I loved it.

I felt my heart skip a beat. "Does that mean..."

He bit his lip and looked away. "Yeah." Then he sighed and whispered, "But...if you change your mind I understand. I'm not worth anything, and...if I disappoint you–"

"Don't think like that." He glanced up at me and smiled a little. I leaned down–

But Steff came back. Really, brother? You just had to come back now?

"Bon appetit!" He announced with a smirk. I glared as he set our food down. I decided to stay seated by Nate and began eating, whilst glaring, whilst holding Nate to my side. Yeah, I can multitask.

Steff looked at Nate with a knowing look in his eyes and I saw him blush some more and nudge a little closer to my side. On the other hand, Steff can be really useful!

"Well, I'll be leaving now...Mr. and Mr. Kenneth." This time I choked on the pasta I was eating and began laughing, like, really, really hard.

Nate covered his face with his hands and shook his head slowly. "Oh my god..." He muttered.

I hugged him and nuzzled my face in his hair. He lifted his hands arm awkwardly, not knowing what to do with physical affection. "You know what Nate?"

"What?"

I wanted to say it, but decided it could wait. Even if I've been feeling it for a while now, this must be a lot for him. "Nevermind, I'll tell you later."

Chapter ~Nineteen~

:~*NATHAN*~:.

He drove me home after. What the hell is wrong with me?! I bit my lip as I thought back to when I agreed to be his...partner.

How am I supposed to act? So Kristy was right...surprisingly. Why does he like me? What if...what if he doesn't like me after a while? Just the thought made my chest ache. It's too late for me. I've ignored it for as long as possible, but it's impossible to ignore now. I feel safe with him, and comfortable. He's annoying and bipolar but he took care of me. I think about him when I should be focused on homework, and I want him to keep holding my hand. I don't want him to disappear. That alone is a lot to ask for, right? Was it wrong to wish for that kind of life?

We got out of his car and he slowly led me up to the door, while holding my hand.

"Nathan?" He said.

"Yeah?"

He leaned down and gently pushed his lips to mine. I was slightly shocked, but realized this was, what, the third time we kissed? It felt...wow. It felt...

I kissed him back. He cupped my face and pulled me closer. It felt so right. He trailed his tongue across my lip and I gasped, stepping back. He took advantage immediately and gently pushed me against the door.

He pulled back only slightly to ask, "You okay?" I nodded silently. I had never kissed someone like this before. I probably wasn't any good.

"Please don't tell me Kristy's been giving you tips..." He whispered as he leaned in again and continued. I smiled a little. She would, but I always ran away when she got into detail about her dates.

He moved away from my lips and gave light butterfly kisses down my neck. It was exhilarating, and nothing at all like Mattson. I felt teeth, and jumped when he bit down.

"R-Ryder–don't–" I felt his tongue and gasped.

He made a sound and brought his lips back up to mine. He pulled away at last and we were both breathing deeply. He kissed my forehead.

"Here." He handed me an envelope.

"What...?"

"Forty dollars for each hour we spent together today." He shrugged. "And a little extra."

"Ryder." I whispered. "I cannot take this. This is your money, and–"

"I love you."

My mouth dropped a little and my heart stopped. He smiled warmly and kissed my cheek. "See you at school."

I watched him, speechless, as he skipped to his car, got in, and drove away. I shook my head and opened the white envelope.

Woah.

"What the..." I whispered. He was right. There were over three hundred in the envelope.

I shook my head. That idiot. I have to do all that I can to thank him tomorrow at school. I entered my house with a large grin on my face.

As soon as I opened the door, a huge force drove into my stomach. I coughed and fell to my knees.

"Well..." I looked up at the shadowy figure. "I heard you've been wasting your time, flitting around with 'friends', when your payday was coming up."

My payday?

No.

No, no, no!

Please, god, don't tell me–

"It's the thirty-first, Nathan." Mr. Steven kneeled in front of me. The light from the street lamp lit his ugly face with yellow light and shadows. He grinned and I felt my body wither.

"Pay up."

Chapter ~Twenty~

•

"Don't tell me you forgot?" He gasped in mock surprise.

"Please, I haven't–!" He punched me again and I fell to the side. "Mr–" He kicked my stomach making me unable to speak, or breathe for that matter.

"No excuses Nathan." He smirked. "I hear you've been wasting your time with someone, Nate. Taking money from other's is cheating. Maybe I should meet this Ryder Kenneth and politely ask him to stay out of our little game."

I felt my heart ache. "No..." I whispered. "Don't...How do you...who–"

"I have my sources." He reached down and grabbed my neck. Just this touch caused my muscles to cramp and shake. "That was quite a show you put on out there. I guess you've grown a lot while I was away."

I gasped as he threw me against the couch. "I have money! There–"

He walked over to the box I kept all of my savings in. He grabbed the envelope as well and counted the money.

He took less than a minute to count it all. I closed my eyes and prayed for it to have reached the goal.

"You have enough for rent. But you're short on on the monthly loan payment."

In that moment, I knew I had lost, once again. I whimpered and shook my head. Not again, please not again–

"Not even with the help of your friend. Shame." He tossed the money to the side.

"Don't be sad. I'll give you two weeks. Have all the money by then."

Was...was he serious? I looked up at him almost in fear. The fear had good reason to be there, too. When I looked at his face I saw the smirk that I hated. There was a catch.

"But I still need a small compensation. Before we...begin, I have one more demand." He grabbed my head and brought it close to his face. "How would you like it if I made Ryder disappear, so you would be able to focus on repaying the debt?"

I shook my head frantically, "No, please don't, he has nothing to do with it, I–" He clenched my jaw tighter and I shut up.

"Fine. Then this is what you do. You disappear. Don't think about him, don't talk to him, don't ask for help. You will stop seeing him completely. Unless you want him to have an accident. Got that?"

I felt a tear roll down my cheek. I would never forgive myself. This is all my fault. Ryder, I'm sorry. I'm so, so sorry. I told you, you would be disappointed. He could easily ruin Ryder's life. I nodded slowly.

He smiled. "Good."

Then he grabbed my arm and yanked me off the couch. I could barely catch myself as he yanked me down the hall toward my room. Dread settled throughout my body. Not again...I whimpered. It's happening again.

All I could think about was Ryder.

Even as he tossed me on my bed and trapped me under him, I could only think of him. My boyfriend...that I was betraying...

"Just beat me up, please." I whimpered. "Not again..."

"It just doesn't seem to have the same effect." He smirked. "Or pleasure."

He lowered himself and I tried to thrash at him but he's done this before. He's used to pinning my arm above my head. The whole time I shook and tried to push him off of me.

He ripped my shirt off and all too soon the trembling returned with full force. He unbuttoned his own shirt with one hand and grinded forcefully down. I whimpered and squirmed but I could feel him pushing through his clothing.

It was disgusting.

He was disgusting.

I was disgusting.

Even as he bit my neck and nipped me, it hurt and horrified me. I was too scared and weak to do anything.

Ryder...

On reflex, and as my final protest,, I jerked my knee into his groin. He groaned and glared at me darkly. "Oh Nathan, you know better than that."

His fist pummeled my stomach so I could no longer move, and he easily dominated. I tried screaming, but it was useless. He gagged me with whatever he had, and flipped me over on my back.

Tears streamed down my face as I cried.

-

-

I woke up at the ungodly hour of six. Immediately the events of last night flashed through my head, making me sit up fast. I groaned as a huge headache appeared. Something churned in my stomach and I stumbled to the bathroom before falling over and throwing up everything. I hurt all over.

I didn't look at my reflection. I knew I was ugly. I wiped my mouth and stepped in the shower, cleaning my self and anything left from last night.

Mr. Stevens was gone.

I had two more weeks.

I stepped out of the shower and pulled my clothes on. After looking down at myself, I felt insecure and pulled on a huge jacket. My own jacket. I shoved Ryder's in my school bag and headed out the door. Why did I ever get involved with that guy? It was hurting more than the bruises from last night.

"Nathan, what happened?" Kristy inspected my face carefully when I arrived at work.

"Nothing, really." Good thing she couldn't see the rest of my body. She moved to touch a bruise but I flinched and headed straight for the kitchen, where I stayed for an hour making the day's goods. When it came time for school I left quickly and ran all the way.

When I got there, I slowed down. Immediately I saw Ryder, leaning against my locker. He was handsome. I felt my insides burn with hate and sorrow. How could I do this to him? He saw me and smiled that amazing smile. My legs moved against my will toward him.

"Hey Nate." His smile slipped when he saw my blank expression. "What's wrong?"

I felt like crying, but instead I pulled out his jacket and shoved it at him. He frowned and blinked at me.

"Nate?" He asked again

All right. Now or never. I can do this. I'm sorry Ryder.

"You're so stupid." I muttered. His expression turned puzzled.

"What?"

I love you.

"I hate you."

His smile vanished and he whispered, "What are you talking about?" He reached to touch my arm but I stepped back hurriedly. Great, as soon as I got over being touched, the fear returned.

"I can't believe you fell for it." I scoffed. It was a time like this, that I hated myself for being such a good liar. I grinned and continued the act. "You really were the easiest among everyone to fool."

He stared at me in surprise. "Fell for it...? What are you talking about? Are you okay?"

He moved to caress my face and despite myself, I jumped back. "You're dumber than I thought. Don't you get it? I don't like you. I never did." I love you.

"You're lying. We're literally going out. Last week...yesterday–" He said.

I rolled my eyes. "The money, Ryder. Think for a moment. I did it for the money. And you fell for it. Thanks, by the way, it was easy."

His eyes were wide and shocked.

"You're lying." He whispered. It surprised me when his face turned into one with determination. "I know you are."

"I used you, don't you get it?"

"You hate money! You said so yourself, 'I'm not the kind of person to take money like this.' I know you Nathan. I know you're lying."

"I'm not lying." I whispered.

"Then why are you crying?"

I touched my face in shock and true to his word, the tears had slipped. I was crying. I can't be weak like this. I need to say something so he'll believe me, so he'll hate me.

"Don't touch me!" I screamed when he touched my arm. I gripped my elbow. His hand froze.

"Are you...scared of me again?" He said, his face falling apart.

If I can't push him away...

"You're a fucking idiot. It's because you're disgusting. Stay away from me fag." I spat and pushed past him.

I hate myself.

Chapter ~Twenty-One~

:~* NATHAN *~:.

•

Just kill me now.

I wiped away the tears that threatened to cascade over and ran out of math before Ryder could stop me. He's been hounding me all day, but when I caught his eye before class, he looked away first. Like there was too much in his brain and he couldn't make sense of anything. I took advantage of the fact he had trouble processing his emotions. He must have told Marcus, because he was also trying to track me down.

A few weeks ago, I thought Mr. Stevens had driven my life as off course as it could get, but now? It was worse. I'm hurting him, the person I want nothing more but for him to stay by my side.

Despite that, I ended the tutoring. I told Ms. Richmond straight up and she tried to talk me out of it, but I knew that was out of the question.

But money I was getting from tutoring was what helped me get almost enough for payday, so without it, I stood no chance at reaching the set day in two weeks. I was finished if I didn't get a new job.

When school ended, I bolted.

.:~* RYDER *~:.

He was just playing a huge, sick joke and was lying. I knew he could hide things pretty well, but...what he said, it tickled me wrong. Nate wouldn't have said that, at least the Nate I knew and loved.

My heart was shattered. He wouldn't look at me, he called me the very word he couldn't stand hearing. He recoiled at my touch. Even if he was lying, I must have done something. I must have hurt him, or done something he wasn't ready for.

"He called me a fag." I whispered for the nth time to Marcus. He rubbed his face with his hands and groaned.

"But...Ryder, I seriously don't believe that Nathan, of all people, could turn on you like th–"

"He said it was a lie. He said he wanted my money. This morning he..." I shook my head in disbelief. It hurt simply saying it.

"I think something's going on. I don't believe it."

"He said so! You don't believe me? He cussed, he called me a fag, he...he..." I punched my bedroom wall. I tried to quell the anger that was burning up inside. It wasn't at Nathan, how could I be angry at him. But I didn't know where it was coming from.

"Dude!" He ordered. He scratched his head and closed his eyes. "Ryder, I believe you when you say he said all that stuff. What I don't believe is that he said he would be your boyfriend, then dump everything down the drain the next morning."

"It doesn't make sense." I muttered. "Because if he used me–" I stopped. He wasn't like that. But he was so convincing. It wasn't fair that he could lie so well to my face. It wasn't fair that he wasn't relying on me. Again and again, I replayed the way he yanked away from me and called me disgusting. "Either way. He doesn't want me by his side. Stay with him, please Marcus? Just watch over him when I'm not there. He still needs someone during school. I need to find out if he was telling the truth. Even if I get mad, stay by his side, okay? I gotta go."

I slammed the door on my way out.

"Ryder!" Marcus shouted after me but I ignored him. I needed to think. I didn't understand what I was feeling or thinking. I was mad that Marcus could so easily believe Nathan was lying, whereas I can't. He wasn't there. He didn't see Nathan's reaction. It's better this way. I can't be by his side half-heartedly like this.

"Ryder, what's wrong?" My mom asked on my way out.

"Nothing." She touched my arm but I slinked away and out the door. She would take his side and say I'm making a fuss over nothing. And I'd want to believe her, but it would only make me feel shittier for doubting him. God, I'm the worst. I'm the most worthless human on the planet right now.

I breathed out. What am I supposed to do now? I flipped open my phone and got a jolt of sadness when I found no missed calls, from a particular person. I yelled and kicked a tree.

I scrolled through my contacts and pressed the call button for that asshole.

"Hey Jonah, I have a question."

.:~* NATHAN *~:.

"What did you say to Ryder?!" Kristy half-yelled at me.

"What?"

"Please tell me you did not call him the f-word and dump him."

"What if I did?"

She grabbed my shoulders and held me face-to face. It was hard looking into her eyes and keep a straight face. "He loves you."

I rolled my eyes. "He doesn't–"

"He does. And you love him. And you two finally got together. So why the hell did you say all that to him!?"

I pushed her away. "I don't like him. I was planning this ever since he came here with his mom. Go back to work, I'm busy." I raised the newspaper to show our conversation was over. Apparently I wasn't the decider of that, because she continued talking until one of the customers came and she had to take the order.

I sighed and searched through the paper some more. None of the jobs here hired people my age. I might as well work at those cheap bars I heard of that don't follow regulations who pay under the table. At least they have good pay...

Wait.

I'm stupid.

I slammed the paper shut and didn't bother changing out of my work clothes before grabbing my stuff and darting out of the café. My shift was over anyway. I ran and caught the bus that was about to leave. The district over had this run down place that had popular clubs and bars.

One problem. I hate alcohol. And bars. And of everything about drunk people. All those things combined are going to send me into a nightmare. But...that's the only job I know that might hire me. I mean, there's still the chance they won't hire me, so there's nothing to lose...right? I gulped and got off the bus.

I remember Mr. Steven talking about a shabby but popular one he hated because they mixed the drinks too much. I finally found it near the back in a graffiti walled building. I looked up with disdain and forced my feet to continue moving.

Instead of going through the front where a large man in dirty clothes watched the people coming in and out, I hurried around to the back. It stunk of alcohol and trash. I covered my nose and shut the rusted door behind me.

There was a dull thrum of music. As far as I knew, there was only the main pub out front and the office of the owner. I headed there first and tried to ignore the peeling of paint and signs of fights.

My breathing caught in my throat when I saw a slumped figure against the wall, unconscious and with a bottle in his hand. I edged around him and practically ran to what I thought was the manager's office. I breathed deeply and told myself I have to do this, it's my last resort, and knocked.

"Who is it?" A voice called from inside.

Well, they didn't sound drunk. "U-um...I...I'm here to ask about a job?"

There was silence before lots of shuffling and moments later the door swung open. "Hello there! Come in."

I blinked at the man in front of me. He was pretty tall, and had long blond hair tied back. He smiled like we were playing a game and motioned me in.

I sat opposite him at his desk. He leaned across and said, "Now, who are you? I don't remember putting up a job listing, but I'm always open to hiring."

"M-my name is Nathan." I stuttered, still unsure of what I was doing.

"Nathan, relax. Call me Robin. Please, tell me why you want a job," His smile dropped slightly as his eyes gazed at me over his moon glasses, "at such a young age?"

I blinked twice. I got the feeling he was a whole lot more mature than he sounded, and older than he looked. "I just need to earn money to get by, and...there's not many people that accept people my age." I whispered softly.

"Aw!" He clasped his hands together and I swear his eyes sparkled. "Nathan you're so cute! I almost don't want to hire you now!"

My eyes widened a little. "Why not?"

He smiled a little sadly. "Do you understand that if I hire you, you will be working the bar? Mixing drinks and dealing with these drunk bustards all night?" He took off his glasses and pierced me with his hazel eyes. "I can tell, just by looking at you, that's not what you want. You could get hurt. I don't fancy allowing young people like you under such influence."

"But-!" He raised an eyebrow at my outburst and I shut up quickly. "I mean—"

"No, it's fine, yell if you want. That just shows me you really need this job."

I breathed deeply and steadied my voice, looking him square in the eye. "Sir, I need this job. I need to pay this man—"

"Name?"

"What?"

"What's the man's name?"

"...Mr. Stevens..."

He laughed loudly. "Ew! Him!" He sighed and nodded vigorously. "Fine, fine. You got the job."

"Really?" I asked with full surprise.

He nodded again. "Everyone knows him. I banned him. He never ceases to insult my drinks. But, if someone as young as you has a debt to pay off, you must have gone through a lot. Tell me, is your last name Strauss?"

"How...?"

"He talked about you sometimes. And I'm ashamed to say, I know more than I should. TMI, know what I mean?

I stiffened and felt very uncomfortable. Robin stood up and adjusted his collar. He walked around my chair and I stayed absolutely still. "I'll give you a job, on one condition."

"What?" I asked almost silently.

"Get your life back and get away from that bastard."

~~~

"Jus' gemme some beer, thanks." The man tossed a small wad of cash at me and I caught it, slipping it into my apron to later add to the machine.

I poured some of the contents of the pitcher in a glass cup and slid it to him. Another man a few seats away called, "Hey, over here."

"Coming." I muttered and grabbed his cup.

"You're new, aren't you? Why would a young pretty kid like you work in this place?"

I ignored him and his horrible breath and slid him his glass, overly diluted with mixer. Before I could turn to put the money in the register he caught
~~~

my sleeve over from over the counter. My heart jumped but I made sure to stay void of emotion.

"Please let go of me Sir." I said in a monotone voice.

"Acting tough, ah? I like it." He yanked on my shirt and I hit the counter. I tried to snatch my arm back but he smirked and leaned closer.

He's going to...my god, what am I doing! I shut my eyes and tried to lean away.

I felt his drunk breath come closer.

And closer.

And closer.

Ryder. I want Ryder.

"You will get your hand off my underling if you want to keep your balls, bastard." I was wrenched away from the man and my eyes widened. There was a source of warmth next to me, and though I knew it wasn't, I wanted it to have been Ryder that held me.

I looked up at Robin, who was even better at keeping a deadly glare, and I stepped away embarrassed that I needed help.

"Little bitch wants it, don't ya?" He flapped his head in my direction and I mentally plugged my ears and tried not to shake my head too wildly.

Robin stepped away from me, leaned over the counter, and shoved the man off his stool. I was too shocked to move. Most of the people sitting around watched.

"I will say this once," Robin began in a deep daunting voice. He glared at the man, and then glanced sideways to the rest of the crowd. "And all of you will listen. This boy is off limits. He will mix and serve you your drinks. But if you lay even a finger, or speak in any vile way toward him, I will personally castrate you and you will be banned from every bar in this zipcode. Do I make myself clear?" Everyone stared at him with a casual fear like they knew better than to disobey. He glowered and demanded, "I said, do I make myself clear?!"

All at once everyone nodded vigorously.

The next second he perked up with a cheery smile and said, "Good! Now sir, please take your belongings and leave the bar, you are banned for the month. Thank you!"

"Robin..." I whispered and he shook his head.

"Hey now, no worries. I warned you this would happen. You go home for tonight, you'll still get your pay. I'll take over the bar and tomorrow you can start again, okay?"

I looked away and nodded. "Okay."

"Good, go home and stay safe Nathan."

I smiled.

And in my head, all I could think was 'thank you Robin.'

Chapter ~Twenty-Two~

:~* NATHAN *~:.

●

I can't stop yawning.

I finish my shift at The Rose and then head directly to school. Working has been my world for these past few days.

My arms were sore, and there were obvious circles under my eyes. Everyday there was only enough time for, at most, two hours of sleep. But I do get to rest on the bus from the shop to the bar.

Every night I feel like crying. Like breaking down and doing my best to rid myself from this world. But then I would realize I had a shift in an hour, and decided to ...deal with it.

Deal with it Nathan. That's what you did before. That's your only choice now.

I need to make the payday in one week.

I sighed as my head ached with exhaustion. Not to mention, I skipped school today and yesterday to put in extra hours cleaning the bar. Robin protested heavily, but I won out in the end. I was only going to school later today to collect the tons of work I've missed and hopefully be able to do them on the bus.

My thoughts were stashed away when the clink of the bell above the front door reached through the empty café. I readied a large smile and told them "Good morning, my shift is ending but another host is coming in–"

"Haven't seen you with a smile for this whole week, Nate."

...Marcus?

I controlled my feelings and kept a believable, snotty grin on my face. This guy...is too dang persistent. All week he's tried to get a hold of me, whereas even Ryder has finally laid off and been avoiding me.

"I know you're faking it though."

"I'm going." I left him standing there and went to the back, changing quickly and slipping quietly out the back.

Obviously, I wasn't as stealthy as I thought. "Where were you for the past two days? You're not sick are you? You haven't been in school. God, I've been worrying. You have no idea what Ryder is thinking right now. What's going on?"

My heart jumped steadily in my chest.

I knew this was for the best. I knew I brought everything upon myself. I knew this was all my fault. But to know that Marcus, the guy that used to beat me up, the guy that I knew now to be quite nice, was now the only one that still believed I was a good person...it hurt. Ryder hates me. Ryder...Ryder...Ryder...Why do you have to be on my mind when I need to focus on being horrible? When I need to focus on work! Why did it have to be you who I pushed away?

"Nathan, stop."

I halted my stride. I just noticed how heavily I was breathing, and how quick my pace had increased.

Marcus caught up and grabbed my shoulders, leaning down to level our eyes.

"Don't you get it?"

Huh?

"I don't believe you."

Silence.

"And I know you aren't going to tell me anything. But I will help you. And I will fix whatever's going on."

With that, and a final second of intense stare, he broke away and strode past toward the school.

Why?

~~~~~

I didn't see Ryder all day. Now that I think about it, I didn't see Marcus either. It was a sort of painful relief. Now I was walking into the bar ready to prepare for my night shift. This afternoon was torture, which consisted of Kristy giving me the stare throughout my shift. Right when I was about to ask if there was something on my face, a sad look crossed her face and she turned away.

Great. I'm even pushing away Kristy.

The scary part of this evening was that as I sat on the bus and walked the streets, I felt like I was being watched. It was a feeling I'd rather not have. I rushed into the bar and like usual stopped by Robin's office to tell him I
~~~~~

was here. Instead of finding the tall blonde sitting at the desk playing with his pencils like usual, there was a note.

'Hello Nathan! I'll be gone for the evening, sorry for not warning you earlier. We are closing early tonight, so pretty please lock up at ten before you leave and take out the trash. Don't get in any trouble, and your paycheck is in the drawer. Good night!

~^_^~Robin Hood'

...I felt my eye twitch. What the heck was this? I could almost hear his voice reading it giddily, and what's up with the emoticon at the end? And seriously, Robin Hood?

In any case, I pulled out my paycheck and my eyes widened, like...oh my god. I'm so close.

I hurried out to the front of the bar and began serving the wine, beer, and multitude of alcoholic drinks. Although I was pleased at my earnings, I couldn't help but feel slightly exposed tonight. Robin wasn't here, and even though he warned everyone not to bother me, I didn't feel safe without him across the hall.

I willed the evening to go faster. By the end of the night I was itching to get out of there. I just had a bad feeling. With the help of the security guy out front, everyone left without hassle and I was able to lock up.

My (must I add few?) muscles ached as I hauled the trash out the back door. I dragged it down the alley and with a groan hauled it into the dumpster.

I sighed and looked up at the night sky.

The stars shined.

Sadness flowed through me. I wonder why my father killed himself. Why couldn't he kill me completely? Was making me suffer now his way of telling me it was my fault mom died? I wonder if he's happier wherever he is, and if he met mom again.

"Hey babe."

I jumped and swung blindly into the dark behind me. What was that?

Something hard hit my chest and I slammed against the dumpster. I groaned and slid to the ground. The stars were spinning.

"Fuck Robin for getting in our way right?"

Could this man be the one from the day I started working?

I half screamed but bit my tongue as he grabbed me...where I do not want to be grabbed. I finally found my sight and realized it was the guy from before, and the worst part was there were two more men with him.

"Lucky us, being in town the day Robin is gone." One of them snickered.

The second one spoke and kneeled down to pull on my hair, making me squirm against the dumpster, "he's cute."

"Leave me alone." I muttered and shoved the man off of me. I scrambled to the side but before I could steady my feet I tripped and hit the brick wall.

The three laughed and stalked toward me slowly.

What was going on?

"Go away." I whispered. "Stay away!" I was almost to my feet again when the guy I already met grasped my shirt, scratching me in the process.

"Come on slut, show us what you got." His foul breath hit the side of my face.

I gagged and became frantic.

Was it happening again?

Please. Not...not...not...again.

My pale skin, still bruised from earlier treatment, cried in agony as the man roughly felt me over. I whimpered and kicked, pushing my back against the wall. He pulled at my hair and after a moment of pause, asked, "who wants to go first?"

"I think being the guest, I should get the first crack, don't you agree?"

I couldn't tell which was which. All I knew was that they were monsters, different versions of Mr. Stevens. All wanting the same disgusting...thing ......me.

The man was replaced with another and his hands grabbed my hips, pulling me under him. Why was I so weak.... He revealed my wrist and slid his tongue across it, then trailed his hand...down my chest...

And...

...and...

...no-....

...not-......

I screamed. One thought rang through my head. What did I do to deserve this? But all I could do...was scream.

Chapter ~Twenty-Three~

:~* NATHAN *~:.

●

What I didn't expect was to have my scream answered.

But it only came moments later. He silenced my scream with a punch to the jaw, but I could only try to scream more as he bit down on my neck, breaking skin. I cried in agony

His nails scratched my skin as he tore at my shirt...then he reached...f...for–

WHY?! WHY. WAS. THIS. HAPPENING...TO ME?

"NATHAAAN!"

"YOU BASTARDS, GET THE FUCK OFF OF HIM!"

I gasped as a blast of cold air washed my skin where the mans heat disappeared. Suddenly I was free and curled my limp body into the corner between the wall and dumpster. The tears stained my bruised and flushed cheeks and I clutched my wrist and arms against my chest. I didn't dare to look up even when the shouts of profanity were gone. I was shaking where I sat.

Shaking yet frozen to the spot as a footstep fell, slowly, toward where I sat. Slowly...whoever it was...came closer...and closer...till–

Warmth.

Whoever saved me, pulled me against their chest and cradled me. At this point, I was too lost to care.

But there was one thing I was painfully aware of.

It wasn't Ryder.

"Nathan...oh my god..." Marcus smoothed my hair and despite myself I let everything come down. I let everything out with the tears. I was tired of pretending. I sobbed for all that was worth and clutched his shirt. I cried out the pain. "Shh...it's okay. I'm right here. I won't leave."

I whimpered like a pathetic child into his chest.

Why?

Why me?

"Marcus." I whispered after a long time after I finished crying and was just sitting, in need of someone to just sit there and hug me like I mattered.

"Yeah?" He responded and pulled away slightly, giving me space. His eyes were filled with worry and pain.

"I'm sorry."

He smiled in agony and pulled me into his chest. I sighed and realized.

I needed someone to know.

~~~~~~~~

We sat in silence.
~~~~~~~~

I was back in my normal clothes with my huge jacket over my shoulders and sitting on one of the bar stools. Marcus sat next to me with his head in his hands, shaking slightly. He honestly looked pretty pissed.

"You can't call the police because he's got people there, and he'll be back no matter what." He repeated one of the many things I said in my long story. I stayed silent.

"You haven't told anyone about what's recently been happening." Silence.

"And you are living in hell because you love Ryder."

"I don't have a-"

"Choice? You're right." He raised his head and locked my eyes. "You only have one choice."

A minute passed with me staring with despair back at him.

"You only...have one choice. You need to tell Ryder."

"Marcus-"

"Nathan!"

"But Marcus-"

"He LOVES you!" He cried in exasperation that it made my heart stop. "You love him. All you need to do is make him understand. He will forgive you. I know Ryder. He's afraid and he won't admit it. He's afraid the one person he truly loves, had used him. Tell him, before you lose him. His family is powerful too; his dad is a lawyer. He can help you. He...he's the reason I'm here. He told me to check on you because he thinks you're either telling the truth, or that he's traumatized you in some unforgivable way. All you have to do is set things straight."

I looked down at my hands. Could I really tell him?

"Come on." He grabbed my hand and pulled me out to the streets, to where his car was.

"I have a question..." I said softly as I sat almost numbly in the passenger seat.

"Yeah?"

"How'd you know I was here?"

He smiled a little. "I followed you when you left The Rose." I looked at him like he was crazy and he laughed. "I was talking to Kristy, and she told me you've been rushing out somewhere recently. I promised both of them that I would follow you, and make sure you weren't in trouble. Good thing too."

"Thanks..." I mumbled.

"Now hop in. I'm taking you to Ryder." He smiled kindly and I smiled back. Thank you so much Marcus. I wasn't sure that this was a good idea...but...I don't know. I really don't know. I pushed him away so well, was it really worth trying to get him back if it hurts both of us? I had a reason for what I did, and Marcus knows my reasons...but now I was lost. I didn't want to hide by myself anymore. I had to trust Marcus's judgment.

If only Mr. Stevens was gone.

Chapter ~Twenty-Four~

:~* NATHAN *~:.

•

"Are you sure..." I asked for the nth time.

"Just try." Marcus smiled. "Mr. Stevens doesn't know you're here, and I doubt he will be able to find out if you make it quick. It can't hurt to try."

I nodded. He opened the car door and walked me to the house. He said he'd wait in the car. Please let him be right.

I rang the doorbell. It was pretty late, so I'm sure even Marcus was doubting if he was awake. But the door swung open and my heart literally leaped in expectancy.

But it was only Mattson.

He whistled. "Woah, what happened to you?"

I gave a straight face. "I need to talk to Ryder."

"He's..." Mattson stopped, looked over his shoulder, and motioned me in with a smile. "Come on."

I looked at him suspiciously as he led me up the staircase. He stopped a few doors down from Ryders room. I regrettably realized that it felt like forever since I last came here.

"He's in here." He opened the door and I stepped in. But it was just another room, and Ryder was not there. I turned around and raised an eyebrow.

"He's not here?"

Mattson closed the door and walked toward me.

"Yeah, I know."

~~

"MARCUS!" I screamed, but of course he's not going to hear me. I'm two floors up, and he's in the car. My chest was rising and falling about as fast as Mattson moved over me. I had stumbled back into a corner.

"Nobody's home." He rolled his eyes. "Come on, I haven't seen you in a while. Why haven't you been coming over? Did you and Ryder get in a fight? Realized you should just be with me instead of him?"

"M-Mattso-" All of a sudden his cold hand brushed under my shirt, I flinched and bit my lip. He felt around my chest and I yelled, "Mattson!"

He made a sound from deep in his throat and I gulped, literally ready to burst into tears.

"Please Mattson...please, please, please, I've had enough, I can't, I-I...please, you can't..."

Nathan you're pathetic. You are begging, underneath him. But what else could I do? I was already bruised and vulnerable, and tired and weak, and...and...

"Nathan...why are you crying..." I winced as he brushed a tear away and touched the bruise on my face.

"Please Mattson...I can't...I...I-"

"Am I hurting you?"

I just bit my lip harder and squeezed my eyes shut. He's going to do it to me. Just like Mr. Stevens and those guys, Mattson was going to break me.

You're already broken Nathan.

It hurt, it hurt, it hurt!

I felt his lips brush against mine with pressure. I whimpered and dug my nails into the floor, knowing in a moment he will dominate and create his own pleasure. It hurt. Maybe I should just give up.

I should just d-

"I'm sorry." He let his head fall into the crook of my neck. My eyes shot open and stared wide eyed, with tears brimming. "Damn it. I thought I could change your mind. Ryder's who you're in love with, right? I shouldn't...I shouldn't have tried to get in between that. But Nathan, I find you attractive. I like you. I'm sorry for scaring you. I know I can't."

Still shaking from him touching me, and still being on me, I slowly tapped his shoulder. I was tense but ignored it. I was scared but I did it anyway.

"I-I'm sorry Mattson." I whispered. "I'm a horrible person. And...I...I can't give you...what you want. I...I l-love Ryder."

He sighed into my shoulder and raised his head to look at me. He gave a small smile. "I get it."

I stared at him.

He...

He stopped?

He wont do that to me?

"Mattso-"

"What the fuck is going on here."

I jumped up so fast I bumped heads with Mattson's. I looked over his shoulder, with my heart beating a million beats per second.

Ryder looked down at us, at Mattson practically on me. He met my eye.

"Ryder, i-it's not...Ryder I-"

"Fuck you."

My heart stopped. He glared at me with so much sadness and hurt but most of all, the thing that hurt me the most...

Hate.

Anger.

He hates me.

I was supposed to tell him everything tonight and fix it. How could this happen? This misunderstanding... please Ryder...

Mattson hurriedly fell to his side, casting me a look that explained this was not his intention. I got up and stood in front of Ryder.

"Mattson and I were not...you know I can't do that. I came to see you. I-I was lying. Ryder I-"

"No shit you're a liar." I winced. "Damn it!" He punched the wall and I jumped away. I really had hurt him. And now he probably thinks I just tried to be with Mattson. Please God, please help me.

"Ryder...please let me explain..." I whispered and took a step forward.

He glared and shoved me back. The place his hands touched my arms stung with want and rejection. "No. I get it now. You were telling the truth. You were just using me, Nathan."

I felt tears clog my throat. "I...it's not...like...that. I–"

"Shut up." He said and I ...couldn't do anything. "You used me Nathan. Jonah told me he's seen you do the exact same thing with some other guy, but even then I believed you. And now you...fuck. I get it already. I don't want to see you either! You are so much fucking trouble. I can't think straight, and you're just being a shitty, fucking, whore, going around to whatever guy you see. I can't believe I actually fell for you and all your lies! Well you know what? It's a shame I've ever met you! It's a shame you didn't die when your dad tried to kill you. Your parents must be glad where they are because youre not there to fucking ruin it-!"

There was a loud crack and silence fell around us.

All you could hear was the breathing of the person who was yelling.

And the breathing of the person crying.

"I..."

His stormy grey eyes were wide in shock, his head forced to face the side.

"I..."

The red mark on his check from where I slapped him bruised his skin.

"I..."

He finally turned slowly to look at me. Even with the mark...Ryder was beautiful. And in pain.

"I'm sorry." I cried.

So many emotions passed across his face, and after only a second I couldn't bear to look him in the eyes. I shouldn't... "I..."

I shouldn't have came here...

I shouldn't have let Ryder get so close.

When I knew this would happen.

That both of us would get hurt.

"I'm sorry." I whispered in agony. I ran past him, unable to avoid our shoulders touching on the way out. The tiny contact sent full shocks throughout my body and I screamed on the inside.

I flew through the house. I wanted to slam the door shut behind me but it came out as a weak push and it barely made a click.

I couldn't take even one step toward Marcus' car before I broke down and collapsed against the wall. My mouth opened to scream with all my might but you couldn't hear it. It was a silent scream. My hands balled up and pulled my hair. I sobbed hard.

It hurt.

How could he...

No. How could I...

I felt myself engulfed. I knew it was Marcus. He just hugged me. I buried my face in his chest and screamed.

And screamed.

Until he picked me up and set me in the car. I rolled up against the door and continued to cry.

He didn't say anything. He started the car and began driving home. I felt like letting another silent scream pour out, but all of a sudden I was too tired. I watched as the street lights passed, only staying around for a second before moving on.

The car stopped. Kristy must have given him my address.

He came around and picked me up again gently, entering my open house.

He walked down the hall, peeking into the rooms until he found mine. He set me down in my bed and pulled the blanket over my shaking body. He pet my head and let his anger very visibly pour from his eyes.

"Nathan I..." He started. I shook my head, telling him it's fine. "That idiot. I'll talk to him."

"He hates me Marcus." I whispered in a monotone voice . There was no point anymore in trying to convince him. "Just leave it."

"He's just confused, I will talk to him, you need help Nat–"

"I don't." I shook my head some more and looked away. "I...just leave me alone. Please."

His eyes were guilty as he closed his mouth. He nodded and sighed. He was about to leave and said, "Don't give up Nathan."

And finally I was left alone in the dark and in silence with small tears traveling and wetting my pillow.

Five more days.

This is the last time, I decided.

There really was no point.

If I can't pay Mr. Stevens again, and I have to go through that again…I will make it my last. I know after that I wouldn't be able to take any more. I will end everything completely, and not even the best doctors will be able to bring me back.

That was a promise. And I intended to keep it.

Chapter ~Twenty-Five~

AN: Hi everyone! I hope you are all doing well and hanging in there. Remember to relax your shoulders, unclench your jaw, relax your eyebrows, breathe, and drink water!

~

.:RYDER:.

Damn it. Damn it all.

I didn't know what to do.

I had thought, how dare he! After what he did, even after I defended him when Jonah tried telling me that he's been with another guy before, he just...he just came over and was ready to play Mattson! In my house!

That crossed the line. I got so mad, and I was ready to punch a whole through the wall. Or Mattson would do.

I snapped. I was the one that hurt him this time. I failed to control myself. Whether he was telling the truth or lying, I was supposed to bear with it and keep it together.

I meant everything except what I said about his dad. I internally cringed at myself. I didn't mean it. I'm the worst.

Why did I say that about his dad? How could I have said he should have died so we wouldn't be in this position now? No one, no one should be told that! Yet I did.

Then he slapped me. Nathan slapped me.

And it hurt inside and out. I wish he hit me again and again. I deserved it.

But then I would remember what he did. And why he was here. And the irrational anger would come back. The hate.

"I'm sorry." It felt like there was so much more behind those words, and so much he was thinking and wanted to say. But that's all he could say.

It felt like he was saying he was sorry for being alive.

Then he left. I felt shocks when his shoulder touched mine.

Nathan, what happened? How did it come to this?

"You fucker." My head snapped to the side and I groaned, holding my hand to my jaw. I glared at Mattson rubbing his fist with a murderous glare on his face.

"What the hell bastard?" I swore. The storm in his dark eyes lit up and he jabbed a finger at my chest and shoved his face close.

"Me? You are the bastard here. I was the one making a move on him. But you know why I stopped? Because he wouldn't let me. Because he was scared. Because he's going through something fucking terrible, and he would never touch anyone but you! Because he loves YOU! I don't give a flying fuck what happened between you two. You are the asshole. You are a dick, but you still need to grow some balls and face him because you are obviously misunderstanding something."

With that Mattson shoved past me, muttering, "I quit."

In a minute I heard the front door slam. My lips were parted in shock and I swear I could hear the pounding of my heart.

I wasn't misunderstanding anything.

But then he...why Nate...Marcus...Mattson...why...DAMN IT!

There were too many thoughts coming through my head! It was too confusing. If he wanted out I was going to let him. He didn't have to go this far. This is the end of it. We were over. It was all over. I shouldn't think about it any more. His games are none of my business.

I looked at my reflection in the mirror across the room. The red mark he gave me was slowly fading.

I don't care anymore.

But it sure as hell still hurt.

.:~* NATHAN *~:.

"What's going on?" I asked Kristy a little distractedly.

She was just staring at me and looked about ready to either hug me or strangle me. It was hard to tell. Dang it, what if Marcus told her—

"We're getting ready for this thing tonight, but seriously, who throws a party on a Monday? We're catering and serving at the party. So are you. Only a few people will be working it, so you'll be paid at least a hundred for a couple of hours."

"A hundred? Really? Just for tonight?"

"Yeah...and here's your pay check for the week since we'll be closed tomorrow."

Great...this should help a lot. Before I got to work I called Robin at the bar, telling him I wont be coming to work tonight. He seemed pretty ecstatic I was taking a night off, until I told him about my plans. Then he began whining.

"Okay I'll be there."

"Nathan..." Kristy whispered.

"Yeah?"

Her face scrunched up and she looked away. She gave me a playful shove to the tables that were waiting to be served. "I don't understand...why you have to go through so much."

I stared at her monotonously. Had Marcus...? No...yes? I don't know. So in response I smiled. "Go through what? I'm fine."

"Liar."

I could have reassured her I was awesome and nothing was wrong and my life was perfectly normal, as usual. But I couldn't. So I smiled and walked away to the tables waiting for me.

"Good morning and welcome to the Red Rose. My name is Nathan and I'll be your host. What would you be having today?"

~

~

"Sorry Ms. Richmond." I handed her the half complete worksheet. "I didn't finish last nights homework either."

She sighed and took off her glasses, rubbing her eyes. "Nathan, what is going on? You haven't turned in anything for the past week, and you look like a walking skeleton. Is something going on I should know about?"

I shook my head. "Nothing, I've just been distracted lately."

You know. Distracted. That's it. Distracted with making enough money to pay back a sadistic man. Distracted by the hours I spend working, day and night. Distracted by the first person I've ever opened up to hating and ignoring me to the best of his ability. Pain tends to be a little distracting.

She sighed. "And what about your project with Ryder and Marcus?"

I completely forgot about it. "I...we..."

"We haven't been able to work on it. Soccer stuff." Marcus intervened and I breathed with relief.

She sighed again and shook her finger at us. "Just because you guys are good students, I'll extend it one more month. But that's it, and I expect it to be good."

Marcus gave a mocking salute. "You got it, Ms."

We left the class. Marcus gave me a "look" and shook his head. "Nathan–"

"No. Whatever you're going to say, no."

"But Nathan–!"

"Bye."

I got two steps before I felt him grab my shoulder. I tried to pry his hand off but he didn't budge. "Nathan. Don't give up."

I stared at him and squinted my eyes, clenching my jaw and strangling the bag strap in my hand. "Don't give up?" I stepped away, making him let go of my shoulders. "Give up on what? School? Normality?" I whispered, "Ryder?"it.

He breathed out deeply. "All of those." He tossed me something. "He was going to give this to you. I stole " He gave a small laugh. "We're not giving up on you either. We want you to have a life. You'll get your chance. You better or Kristy will kill anyone who gets in your way." He smiled, as if he wanted me to use that as a sign of hope.

I looked down at the box. Marcus nodded and walked away.

It was white with a black ribbon, and fit in the palm of my hand. I couldn't open it right now, maybe later.

Enough of this. I need to return to how I was before. I need to. Otherw ise...otherwise I'm sure to give up. I need to meet this payday, just to save myself for a month. Then I'll return everything to normal. I'll keep the two jobs, and continue picking up odd jobs on the weekends. I'll ...I'll study harder so I can get the scholarship I originally wanted, so it could take me away from here. I'll focus on that, and I'll go back to normal.

I'll forget everything.

If I had a choice, that's what I'd choose.

~

~

"Hurrrryy Nathan we're late!" She shoved a tray at me. "Go! Smile!"

God I hate parties. I mean, I've never really been to one. But I know about it. Loud music, people dancing strangely, and food.

I felt so degraded as I shifted through the crowd of teenagers. Even though I was pretty sure half of them went to my school, I didn't bother trying to remember. No one knew me. Good. What mattered was that the pay was good.

But then something really disturbing approached me. I mean, I'm pretty sure it was a girl, but I wasn't sure. Her make up was all over.

"Waiter, wanna dance?"

"U-uhm s-sorry, excuse me. I'm gonna go...refill this tray." I stepped away hurriedly and bumped into something, and I prayed I didn't just hit a wall. What kind of sane teenager would want waiters at a normal party? Stupid fancy rich people. This guy didn't even look like a teenager–

"Watch where you're going boy! This suit cost me more than you're being paid–"

I watched as he dusted the spilled samples off his coat.

My tray clattered to the ground, the sound of metal against wood ringing in my ears. My breathing stopped entirely and I felt the blood in my cheeks drain.

Nathan. Move. Now.

"And here I thought his party would be less wild than the last one. Damn I spilled my beer..."

Nathan. Now! RUN!

The man finally looked up. My feet didn't budge. I didn't move a muscle.

He smiled. Then chuckled. Then began laughing like crazy. He's drunk.

Finally my body woke up and I whipped away toward the kitchen. He grabbed my wrist.

"Nathan?"

"What are you doing here?" I whispered.

"Hm, it's my nephews birthday. I think I have a right to be here. Did you want to see me?" He brushed my chin and I yanked away.

"I'm working." I cringed. "L-let go."

"Working?" He laughed some more. I tried to swallow but felt the terror rising throughout my body. "What a good boy. But how many times do I have to tell you..."

He grabbed my tray, dropping it on a nearby stand. I didn't know how to respond. What do I do? Do I run? Do I scream for help? Do I hit him over the head with a plant? "You'll never be able to pay it off."

But every one of those options would bring me immeasurable pain in the future. He grabbed my wrist, digging his nails into the vein and forcibly tugged me to the stairs.

"Come on, the real party's up there." He slurred.

"Mr. Steven, I'm working–" I squeaked almost silently. He threw me in front of him into a room and I distanced myself from him as far as I could, which, unfortunately, wasn't very much.

"M-Mr. Steven I–"

"Nathan, shut up. We need to talk." He advanced toward me and I felt as if my entire body shrunk to a useless frail twig. He grabbed my arm and twisted it behind my back. I gave a small scream which was drowned almost completely out by the thumping of music and tried to push him away. He twisted it some more and the pain ripped along my side. It was because he's drunk. He can't handle his alcohol at all. He does what he wants.

This was not what was supposed to happen tonight. Tonight was supposed to go smoothly, absolutely nothing should have happened.

My knees buckled and I fell forward on my face and knees on the bed. The bed dipped as he straddled and continue pressing my arm against me.

Why was he doing this? I had time. I had no idea he was here. Why was he here? He knows he can't do anything unless I fail. H-he...he's not supposed to—

I winced as his other arm came around and rubbed against me.

I yelped and shut my eyes as beads of sweat matted my hair down. "Stop. ..please...you can't, you just...agh!" I cringed again. "Stop!"

Get off. Please, get off.

Can't somebody help me?

He can't he can't he can't!

He can't do this again!

"Uncle, why are you in my room—"

"Stop..." I whispered. He stopped, and looked over his shoulder at whoever it was. I bit my lip in terror, squeezing my eyes shut. I felt him release me and my arm, making me collapse on the bed sheet, cradling my shoulder. I couldn't move. He was going to come back.

I looked to the door apathetically.

"Mattson go back to your party—"

I saw the person look behind Mr. Stevens and found me on his bed, locking eyes. Despite my escalated heart, blood drained from my face. He stared at my helpless, weak form with surprise and confusion.

"Nathan?"

Chapter ~Twenty-Six~

•

I stared back helplessly.

All of a sudden he whipped on Mr. Steven in shock. "What the hell is Nathan doing here?"

"He's just a client. Go back Mattson—"

"What are you doing to Nathan?" He yelled.

Mr. Steven glared stonily at him and walked back to me. I winced as he grabbed my arm and pulled me up.

"Its h ard to believe this wimp is the kid you like. Take my word, he's no fun." Mattson stared at me in confusion and shock. I had just as much idea as he did as to what was going on. But one thing was clear: Mr. Steven trailing his hand absently on my trembling skin.

"stop.." I whispered. His grip tightened as if to tell me to shut up.

Mattson stormed over and shoved him back. He scooped me up as if I weighed nothing. I stared at him and he still looked really confused.

He shook his head. "I'm taking him home."

Mr. Stevens smiled but I could see he was annoyed. "Whatever, do what you like. I wasn't going to hurt him."

Liar.

That was the biggest lie I've ever heard.

Mattson spun on his heels and stalked out of the room with me still in his arms.

"I can walk–"

He didn't respond nor let me down.

He avoided the rooms with people and we went out the back door. He rounded the house and opened the door to an expensive looking car and set me in it. He got in himself and started it up.

"I'm supposed to be working..." I whispered.

He didn't say anything and pulled out of the driveway. Finally I sighed and muttered, "I'm confused."

"So am I." He said in a strained voice. "What were you doing with my uncle?"

I stared at his reflection in the dashboard. "U-uncle?" I whispered. "M-Mr. Steven is your uncle?"

"Yeah." He glared at the road. "What's that to you? How are you connected? What was he doing? He called you his client, what did you do?"

I clenched my teeth and spoke, "I didn't do anything. I never did anything." I shut my eyes and dropped my head in my hands. "I didn't do anything...so why?" I shook my head.

"You're not making any sense..."

I hit my head against the window, making Mattson take a quick glance from the road to me and back. "Why was he there..." I whispered to myself.

"Because it was my birthday...? And it's kind of his house."

I shook my head. The headache called life was pounding against my brain. "Mr. Steven...is your uncle. You're...Mr. Stevens nephew...but..."

"He was touching you."

The silence split my eardrums. Hearing that made my face lose color and made me want to throw up as I thought about what he had seen.

I looked out the window. "I'm sorry." My voice cracked, "I'm a...I'm paying back my fathers debt. I can't...I don't want to say it. I don't want to say anything more." I put a hand over my mouth and squeezed my eyes shut.

Stop being pathetic. You owe Mattson thanks for saving you.

"Does Ryder know."

It was supposed to be a question but the way he said it made my skin crawl, and made a painful memory from a day ago come back.

"He knew about the past. He doesn't know about now."

"What– Nate, this seems serious. My uncle," He sneered, "attacked you. This is Ryder's job, shouldn't he be killing him right now? HOLY SHIT. How long has my uncle–"

"Mattson! Shut up!" I clamped my hands over my ears. "I'm doing my best, I swear I'm doing my best. I will pay him back and he wont own me anymore. Ryder...he was going to do something to Ryder, so I lied and got him away from me but ...but..."

I breathed deeply, Mattson murmured, "It's okay, you don't have to tell me–" But I cut him off and forced myself to realize what's happened till now.

"I don't know how he found out about Ryder. I finally made friends. I finally, for a day, had fun." I smiled in horrible sadness. "It hurts. He hates me. I'm scared. He could have helped me. But...but Mr. Steven never goes away! He always, always, always gets what he wants from me. How did he find out about Ryder..." I drifted off, whispering to myself.

There was silence.

"I told him."

I turned my eyes up at the boy next to me. His knuckles paled as he gripped the wheel and he stared in realization out the window.

"I didn't know he knew you. But...I talked to him about you. About how annoying it was that you only looked at Ryder. And how you guys were obviously together. I didn't know...Nathan I'm so sorry. I didn't know anything. I knew Uncle Steve did pretty suspicious things with a lot of people and money. But I didn't know, I swear, I never meant for him to go after you–"

"He would have anyway." I stared out the window again.

So that's how.

"Nathan I'm sorr–"

"It's okay." I said. "You didn't know. It's okay."

"I'll make it up to you. I'll make him leave you alone and you can get Ryder back–"

"No, please don't. He wont stop. You can't do anything." I pointed down a street where my lonely house was.

"Yes I can, or...I can talk to Ryder? Maybe–"

"Don't tell anyone. The police can't get anything on him. Ryder wont believe you. I'll pay him back this month, and he wont be able to do anything." But I rubbed my wrist, wondering if that was true.

He pulled to a stop in front of my house.

"Thank you." I said. "If he...did something tonight I...When he's drunk...he doesn't think."

"I know." He said back.

I opened the car door. I felt so unfinished leaving the car, like I left with half a story– which I kind of did. "Don't tell anyone." I said again and he sighed.

"Is there anything I can do? At all? I messed a bunch of things up; there must be something. I want to help you."

I looked back at my house and shook my head and smiled. "I'm fine."

He shook his head. It didn't matter if he believed me. I entered the house and shut the door and watched his car disappear down the street through the window.

With my back against the wall I slipped to a sitting position on the floor, with my hand over my mouth. Oh god...

It almost happened again.

Chapter ~Twenty-Seven~

:~* RYDER *~:.

•

I checked my watch. Obviously Jonah and Marcus were taking their sweet time meeting me. I tossed my bag onto my back and decided to wait one more minute. I needed to talk to Marcus about the project for Math. We got nothing done so far. Plus, the last time we met, it was Nathan getting the work together. I'm pretty sure...he doesn't give a shit about the project anymore. I told Marcus we should just do it ourselves. He agreed, but said only because he didn't want to force us together in the same room.

Gee, how considerate.

I was about to enter the building, tired of waiting for my friends, when this pretty nice car rolled into the parking lot. I got a strange feeling in my stomach and followed it with my eyes.

The people that came out made me sick. I forced myself to breathe in and out, and not march over there and pick a fight.

Mattson kept his eyes trained on Nathan as they got out. Nathan continued walking, and didn't seem to see me.

They came to school together.

Nathan and Mattson.

This should probably be nothing, right? It is nothing. Mattson was just a bother to him before, right? There's no way Nathan would be with him. Then again, the other night...what's there to doubt anymore? Just because I wanted to believe him? Just because my gut told me one thing, I was supposed to ignore my eyes and ears?

I clenched my jaw. If he was lying, I had Marcus watching his back, since I was apparently so disgusting and unreliable. If he was telling the truth, he's probably playing his game on Mattons now. I felt my blood boil.

Before he could see me I entered the building and grabbed the nearest girl, who I recalled was one of those that would vie for my attention. A month ago she would have seemed pretty attractive, but now she seemed dull.

"Hey." I said, as if I were "surprised" to see her.

"Hey Ryder." She said, completely turning her back to her friends.

"I heard you broke up with your boyfriend. Must suck."

"Yeah, well, we had other interests. It may have hurt for a while." She gave a cat-like smile. I placed a hand on her shoulder for comfort, and she took advantage of the que. I wasn't like this. But I knew how to do it. She knew what I was aiming for, and probably didn't care if I actually liked her or not; she just wanted the glory.

And what can I say? She was attractive enough not to make me puke.

Out of the corner of my eyes, I saw the front doors open, and a skinny, black haired boy walk in. His gaze was cast at the floor, like an outcast. He wouldn't have seen me if it weren't for the squealing girls to my side.

"Let me make you feel better." I said. I dipped my head down, and closed the distance between our lips.

She responded instantly, and ran her hand up my arms, I cupped her face with my hands. To the world, it would have seemed like a great kiss.

But if felt so, incredibly, wrong.

She was rushing. She was too rough. Her face didn't fit in my hand, her lips were soft but it didn't feel right. She wasn't delicate. She wasn't Nathan.

But I deepened the kiss anyway. She was a good kisser. I opened my eyes ever so slightly and lazily glanced to my right.

He dropped his books. His eyes met mine instantly. He stared.

And I almost tore away from the girl.

It was like watching him die right in front of me. I felt a monster of guilt claw at my chest as I met his eyes. He looked past broken as he stared at me. His body quivered as if he was going to break down– cry and run up to me.

Those dark blue eyes looked at me with pain and tears ready to fall out. Wasn't this the reaction I wanted? I wanted to get him back.

No, I wanted him back. This wasn't the way to do it. I went too far. Holy shit...what am I doing...I shouldn't have done this.

I saw Mattson put a hand on his shoulder and shake him, trying to pull him away. I saw him moving his lips. I mentally slapped myself and glared. If he was mad he would run up to me, slap me, explode with how he really feels. But now I'm just confused, and getting more ticked off by the second. Stop having second thoughts Ryder.

I let my hand slide down her side and she giggled.

Nathan dropped his eyes, and I could no longer see it behind his hair. He ripped away from Mattson and tore down the hall.

At last the girl pulled away. "Thanks, I feel much better." She smiled.

"Huh?" I continued to stare at the place Nathan was standing a second ago.

"Catch you later Ryder." Her friends pulled her away in fits of giggles. A hand bent down to pick up the books I was staring at. I met Mattsons eyes.

I felt myself jump.

Holy crap. He looked like he was ready to murder me. He stared me down with the most hatred I have ever been looked at with.

He walked away and left me, once again, stunned. Why did he look like he wanted to murder me way more than Nathan did? Nathan didn't even look mad! He just looked.... Mattson's face on the other hand, that must've been what I looked like when I caught them together.

I get it. So now he already has Mattson.

I told my legs to start working as I walked in a sort of trance down the hall. I only looked up when I heard a loud commotion. All I saw was a crowd of people laughing and pointing. One of the lockers was open and in a huge mess. Someone must have rigged it, somehow. I never got how you did that. A ton of soda exploded and the victim just stood there facing his locker, soaked.

Then I saw Jonah. Geeze, so this is where he was. Thanks for telling me you got here early—

He grabbed the person by his shoulder and socked him in his stomach. My eyes widened as the person fell against the lockers and slid to the ground. He didn't even raise his arms to defend himself as Jonah kicked his jaw, his sides, his legs. People in the crowd either laughed to fit in or just looked on and rolled their eyes.

Jonah stepped back and laughed.

Nathan just sat there, breathing shallowly, and stared straight ahead with empty eyes.

Jonah shouted to the crowd, "Shows over, move on with your more interesting lives." Everyone listened and began dispersing. I stayed there, because I knew Jonah wasn't finished. He knelt and grabbed Nathan by the chin forcibly.

"Haven't seen you in a while, Strauss." He chuckled. "What's wrong? Can't even protect yourself anymore?"

He cuffed the back of his head and he fell to the side. I didn't realize I was shoving Jonah back, but it happened without much thought. Nathan looked up and met my eyes for the second time this morning.

"Come on man, what the fuck? I told you right? I told you he's been going around like a fag and sucking people off for money. Hah. And you thought you two were friends. Serves you right, fag." Jonahs ugly face smiled back at me, but with hard eyes. "Right Ryder? You said you're done with this piece of shit, right? Prove it."

Nathtans eyes turned away first. In the end, it doesn't matter what the truth is. He hurt me, and I hurt him, and he doesn't want me to protect him. Even if he makes me angry, I don't hate him, but to him, I'm his biggest problem. I turned away and tore myself from his helpless figure.

"Only fags bother with each other, Jonah. So just leave him the fuck alone already or you'll be one too."

Chapter ~Twenty-Eight~

:~* NATHAN *~:.

•

He walked away. The cold look in his eyes told me everything. Jonah glared, laughed, and whispered, "Freak, you heard that right? " He shoved me to my side and stood up, and left me, alone, in the halls. I sat against the lockers with my head rested back, and stared at the ceiling.

I can't do this anymore...

I could see clearly Ryder kissing that girl. He kissed her, and even as he saw me, continued. He looked so cold at me, so angry. Did he see me arrive with Mattson? He wouldn't take no for an answer. Was he mad at me? Didn't he get me back already?

Jonah's fun didn't even hurt as much as seeing Ryder with another person. A girl.

Stupid Nathan. You obviously forgot. He likes girls too. He's popular, and people love him. She was way more attractive than you, everyone is. He probably liked her better than you. She probably kissed better.

That doesn't matter. Nothing matters anymore. I felt myself cry inside when I saw him. He wasn't mine anymore. He wasn't my friend. He hated me. I don't have friends. I'm just an idiot. A mess up.

And this is how it should have stayed.

I stood up. I couldn't go to school today. I walked slowly, afraid of the bruises Jonah gave me. Where could I go? Not home. That would be useless. I need to work. There's only one thing to focus on now, and that was living.

It took two hours to get to downtown. Robin was out front for once, talking to the security. When he saw me, he marched right over and looked down at me over his glasses.

"What are you doing here, Nate?"

"I need to work."

"You should be in school–"

"Robin, please." I pleaded.

"We're only open at night!"

"Let me...clean the bar until tonight. Let me work today. Let me work a full shift tonight–"

"Absolutely not. You–"

"Please Robin." I said. "Please–"

He raised a hand and brushed the bruise on my cheek. I flinched away.

"Something happened." He whispered. He clenched his jaw then sighed, "Fine...But I'm against this, so I'm not giving you an all night shift."

"But–"

"The latest you can stay tonight is twelve." He said firmly. "No objections. Someone needs to give you limits as to how much you can exhaust yourself."

I bit my lip and nodded. He let me into the bar and patted my shoulder. "Why do you look more hopeless than usual?"

I went behind the counter and began grabbing glasses to wash.

"Nathan?"

"It's nothing." I whispered.

"Sure it is." He said. He was in that mature mood he uses when he's serious. No games in his voice. "Nathan?"

I put down a glass. "I..." I thought back to that moment I met his eye. The image of him with that girl burned into my brain. "I just want this to be over."

"Your business with Steve?"

"Yeah..." I whispered. I want everything to be over. It may be a little selfish. People have it worse... people must be suffering worse than me right now. Right? But I'm almost done. Sooner or later, nothing will make sense anymore.

"Don't give up." He walked away, leaving me to think, why were he and Marcus saying that? What am I not supposed to give up on?

~~~

I opened the door to my dark apartment. My hands were raw from cleaning, scrubbing dishes, and then working the normal shift. My legs were jelly because I missed the last bus and had to walk to the next running bus stop, and barely caught that one.
~~~

I collapsed on my bed and groaned. My vision was blurry and my body was extremely fatigued. Old habits die hard I guess. So much has happened in this past week, that it feels like a month has passed; and it's only Tuesday. I can't believe it's only been one week since I hurt Ryder. Now I just have the rest of this week. But I know for a fact...

Today. Was horrible.

I closed my eyes.

"There's no way today could get any worse." I mumbled at myself.

"Was that a challenge?"

I screamed and shot up out of bed. My vision wavered and my heart pounded in my chest. I searched the room for the person who spoke.

"Oh come on, you must be used to this already." And really, I should be. A hand appeared and tried to turn my face but I ripped away and stumbled to the light, flipping it on.

"Mr. Stevens what are you doing here." I whispered feverishly.

He laughed. "Whaaaat? I can't visit my favorite client?" Then he let his real intentions show, and directed his angry face entirely at me. "I'm a little mad you were taken away so suddenly at the party. By my own nephew on top of that. You sure move quick, don't you."

He took a step toward me then stumbled. I looked at the floor where five hard liquor bottles lay. Empty bottles.

I gulped and began stuttering, "W-hy are you here? I have a-n-nother week till–"

"I'm tired of waiting Nate." He yawned and moved toward me. "Why do you even try? You'll never make it. I will always–"

"I will!" I yelled. "I will make it."

He glared and I was immediately intimidated. "I'm changing the deal. Tonight. Right now. Six hundred dollars or you are mine, again, tonight."

I felt my chest tighten as everything came crashing down. My breathing quickened. "You can't do that. You said–"

He grabbed the front of my shirt. "Where is it? Huh? Don't got it? Of course you don't–"

I ripped away from him and ran around the apartment; collecting everything I made this past week. He laughed as my shaking hands almost dropped it all over the floor. I gathered it in my box where the rest of my savings were and handed it to him. I felt my entire life slip away with every dollar he counted. I closed my eyes. I can't believe he was doing this. I hate when he's drunk. He never thinks fair in the first place. He does what he wants and I couldn't do anything.

His face was cast in shadows. "Congratulations."

My eyelids flew open. No way...I felt the corners of my mouth twitch.

"...really?" I whispered.

I made it. I actually made it.

I felt lighter.

He can't do anything for the next–

He threw the box across the room and it slammed against the wall. I jumped back and the money scattered on the other side of the room. He clenched his hands and glanced at me, his eyes were dull daggers.

"Come here."

"What?" I asked, dumbfounded. He grabbed my wrist and I tried to tug away. "What are you doing?" He grabbed my neck and drove me into the ground. "St..." I choked, my mouth opening for breath.

He released my neck but wouldn't move away.

"What are you d...Mr. Steven I gave you the money!"

"Shut up."

"Stop it!" He straddled me and crept his hand across my skin, lifting the shirt as he went. "What are you doing!?" I cried, "Stop!"

"I said SHUT UP!" He backhanded my face. I stared in shock to the side and my blurred vision got the best of me. It was clear enough so I could see him grab one of the beer bottles.

"Get off." I whispered. "Go away. Leave me alone–"

A pain shot through my skull like a bullet as green glass shattered across my face and seconds later, hot liquid trickled across my face and into my mouth.

He reached behind me and let his fingers flutter over a spot on my back, and in response I thrust upward to move away from it. This only resulted in getting me against him. I whimpered and turned my head away but he pulled my hair till I came eye to eye.

His stony gaze told me exactly what he planned on doing.

"I know everything about you." He whispered into my ear. "I know every little trick. I can make you do whatever I want. You are weak. You are nothing. Did you really think I cared about what money I got from you? It was just to give you motivation to stay alive."

He raised the broken beer bottle and raked it down my cheek. I screamed as the pain ripped across my skin.

"I'm rich whether you paid me or not. I don't care at all about the debt your asshole father left. The only thing I thank him for was that he left you to me." He looked down at the button up shirt. "Take it off." I shook my head. He brought the broken and slightly bloodied weapon to my throat and my breath quickened. I internally sobbed as I undid the buttons one by one with hands shaking so violently it made my whole body tremble.

He smiled. "It doesn't matter if you ever pay the debt. I will always get what I want. And what I want is you. There is nothing you can do about it."

Chapter ~Twenty-Nine~

:~* RYDER *~:.

I turned page after page in the yearbook. Stupid, you're supposed to be forgetting about him. But the guilt wouldn't stop making fluttering motions in my stomach. I didn't see him at school today.

Finally I turned the page and found the people who's last name started with S. One more page later and I found his picture.

Nathan Strauss. His hair swept across his face. He wasn't smiling. On some level, it looked like this boy was incapable of showing any expression. On another level, he looked close to tears. I brushed my thumb over the face void of everything. I brought the book closer to my face and scanned it over until I picked up every detail. The sweater pulled tight around his neck. The light shadows under the eyes. The mat of hair. I noticed a shadow under one of the eyes, and for a second I figured it was from his hair. But after further thought, I didn't dismiss the idea of a bruise.

Suddenly I had a weird idea. I kneeled in front of my bed and from under it I pulled out my other yearbooks. I chose the one from freshman year.

I rolled my eyes at my goofy face. Nice picture Ryder. I found his picture and frowned.

Messy hair. Insecure posture. Sad eyes. No smile. This irritated me. I grabbed other older yearbooks. Eighth grade. Seventh grade. Sixth grade. He looked the same. Sad. Lost. Alone.

Fifth grade looked weird. He still looked sad. But he also looked scared.

I didn't even know we've been going to the same school since elementary. I've never heard of him before this year. Our school was huge, but was that possible?

I didn't even want to look at his fourth grade picture. It would just look the same. Little Nathan getting smaller and smaller with a decreasing glint of light in his eyes.

I found Strauss in the yearbook. And he was smiling.

I unintentionally sighed in shock. Hell, he was adorable. He was smiling this childish, knowing smile. A dimple marked one side of his face. I could just imagine the moment. He would see his friends in line behind the photographer, watching, trying to make him laugh. He would bite his lip and mumble at them to stop, before looking back at the camera and grinning like the perfect child.

Comparing that picture to the others, it was hard to believe it was the same person.

Finally I forced myself to forget the idea and shut all the yearbooks, returning them to under the bed.

My phone rang and I looked at the caller.

'Nathan' flashed on the screen. My jaw dropped and my heart stopped. He was calling me? What does he want? I took ten seconds of deep thought before a surge of emotion flowed through me. I pressed answer.

"Hello?" I said.

Unexpectedly there was no answer. I glared at the wall in front of me. "Hello?"

I heard breathing so he was obviously there. My teeth clench. This didn't make sense. Fuck. I don't want to hear his voice.

I moved my finger to the end button.

"Ryder..." A voice finally came through. I tensed up.

"Nathan?"

There was silence. I bottled all the emotions running through me. I will wait. Whatever he wanted to say, I will wait.

"I..."

But after a few seconds, the call hung up. I stared at the phone. Why did he hang up without saying anything? I sat back on my bed and took deep breaths. I pressed the call button, but it went immediately to voicemail.

.:~* NATHAN *~:.

"...love you." I whispered, now to myself. The line was dead. The phone died. I never expected him to actually wait long enough to hear me. I didn't expect him to answer.

But it's okay. All I wanted was to hear his voice. It's okay. If I told him anything, he would only feel worse after this.

I dropped my phone and lay still on the floor, staring at the wall.

I couldn't move.

He left sometime this morning, I don't know when. My body was sore, everywhere, from everything. From him, from work, from school. I hadn't moved all day and the setting sun slowly settled the room into darkness. I could barely stay awake. I tried to sit up but I gasped and collapsed back to the ground, surrounded with glass and blood.

It was disgusting.

I give up.

I lay there. Not moving. Breathing as slow as possible as to not hurt my ribs. After a few hours of slipping in and out of consciousness, hunger started creeping in on me. I winced and swallowed some spit. If I couldn't even pull myself up, there was no way I'd be able to walk to the kitchen.

I felt tears slowly, one after the other, slip down my face. I felt a sob bubble in my throat.

I moved my hand slowly and reached for a large piece of green glass from the broken bottle. I grasped and stared at it, then placed it against my wrist.

I looked at the lines I could have traced years ago.

I pressed it against the fading lines and winced. Stop it Nate, why would you cause yourself more pain?

Because it will make my life go away. It was worth it. I want to die.

I slid it across as hard as I could, and groaned because it didn't go too deep. I felt more tears fall down my face. I tried again. And again.

Suddenly a shoe stomped on my hand and I yelped.

"Nathan...shame on you."

I stared up at him.

"What do you have to say for yourself?"

He pressed against my hand until I dropped the glass, then knelt down and brushed the hair out of my face, "Don't be selfish."

"...why..." I whispered hoarsely. Why would he even...do this kind of stuff with me? Why was he here again?

"Why? Because...you look beautiful when you cry." He gave a drunk laugh and I stared back with tears still pooling over my eyes.

"I hate you..." I whispered past the fear that made my lips tremble. "I–"

He gripped my wrist, the one I had been trying to cut, with force and I cried out. "Hate me? You know, you've been obedient until recently. I think I've given you a little too much freedom. I'm tired of this. For now on, you'll be with me. You've lost your privilege."

"You're drunk..." I whimpered.

He grinned wickedly. "No I'm not." But almost as if to mock me he pulled out a small canteen and took a swig. He chuckled and said, "drink." He put it to my lips but I rolled my head away. He didn't like that. He grabbed my jaw and forced liquid into my mouth. It burned my tongue and scratched my throat. I began coughing and pain shot through my chest. I rolled into myself and he laughed.

"I hope you don't die." He laughed again. He got up and began kicking all the shards of glass out of my reach. He picked up the one I had been using and brought it to my chest.

"You were tracing your scars." He started. He started at the top of my shoulder and brought it slowly across my chest. I shut my eyes and held in the scream. "If you try to do what your idiot father tried, I will make you feel something worse than death."

"I'm already in hell." I seethed to myself. I swear, it didn't even pass my lips. But immediately he grabbed my face and glared.

"This isn't hell. But you will feel it."

My heart rate quickened in fear. His eyes lost some rage as he leaned closer and kissed my temple, trailing down until he pressed against my mouth.

I whimpered and shook my head, or at least tried to. Why? Why would he even want to do anything with me? Look at me! I'm disgusting! In the state I was in, even more so. He cupped my face with his hand and pretended to be gentle. He pulled me closer by my arm and I gripped his shirt, trying to push him away.

He was so rough. He didn't care about what I was feeling through it, or if I wasn't responding. He went too fast. I didn't like it.

"You're disgusting." He whispered into my ear. "That boy was blind to see something in you. Look at you. I hope you didn't honestly think someone could love you."

I know.

"Aren't I lucky he hates you so much now?"

Yeah.

"Have you given up yet?"

Yeah.

"Yes or no?"

Another tear ran off the side of my face as I stared back at him and nodded slowly. He grinned and muttered, "Good boy."

Chapter ~Thirty~

I was breathing heavily. I collapsed on the bed and groaned. I curled into a ball and tried to block out the presence of him stumbling out of the room. Hearing the front door slam close I let myself begin to cry again. The sweat slowly dried, but it would be a while before the blood would crust up.

I stared at the ground where I had laid the day before. At least today I would be paralyzed on the bed and not the cold ground. I weakly grabbed the sheet and pulled it over my quivering body. I wanted to turn over but the pain in my back and hips made it impossible.

I stared out the window. It wasn't raining today.

The sun was high in the sky.

Outside was warm...

My home was cold.

My parents were dead.

My life was spent growing up too soon.

My friends were gone.

My future is gone.

I'm dying.

I wasn't dying fast enough.

I could never go back to normal.

This all happened because of Ryder.

My love hates me with all his heart.

I was alone.

I felt my eyes droop half way close. I was really...really tired. He was going to come back tonight. He kept coming back, every night. Suddenly my ear twitched to a sound in the distance. I could barely comprehend any images, sounds or thoughts. I was going under again. "Nathan?" Was my name being called my someone, or was it my imagination? My body began shaking and my lip quivered. He was back already?

"Nathan!" I heard my name being screamed. It hurt my ear, but it didn't sound like him.

Something yellow entered my bleary vision. A hand touched my shoulder and I wanted to scream at whoever it was to not touch me but the most I could do was cringe away.

"Nathan, oh my god, Nathan. Wake up. Hey, keep looking at me. Oh my God, Marcus look at all the blood. Nathan, I'm so sorry. Look at me." Was that Kristy? She pushed back my hair and patted my face.

"Kristy...his body." I heard someone else warn in a shocked voice. The blanket was pulled down slightly.

I think she muffled her mouth from crying. I closed my eyes all the way. I'm hurting her. Can't they go away?

"Nathan!"

I winced and breathed slowly into my pillow. I tried mouthing, "I'm okay." Suddenly there was a lot of motion.

"Where's your cell phone?!"

"It's been dead since yesterday!"

"Gran has mine...JESUS! Marcus, get the police!"

"I'll get more than the police."

"I'll go...um...The neighbors! Yeah. Oh my god Nathan hold on, you'll be all better in no time. We'll take you to the hospital–"

I felt a tear traveled down my cheek as I shook my head, "no..."

"You have to Nate. It's okay. We'll be right back and will stay with you the whole time. Just...oh god don't move. Just hold on." Less than a minute later silence took over the room once again. Dust floated peacefully where the sunlight melted into my room. It was the middle of the day again.

In all my life, this is the most pain I've ever felt.

I really hope I die. I felt guilty that I might go before I apologized, and thanked everyone, and before explaining to Ryder the truth. He doesn't know my last words. No, it's better than way, remember?

I screamed.

Pain ripped down my back as I was yanked out of bed. Kristy? Marcus? What's going on? A blanket was tossed over my whole body and somehow I was out of my house and lying in a car. I breathed heavily to silence.

I was about to scream for help but for the two seconds I was alone in the car, the emptiness and feeling of being utterly alone in the world cut through my ears like thunder.

No one could possibly help me.

.:~* RYDER *~:.

I spent all morning mentally preparing but he wasn't in school again. I don't know why it made me so irritated. There was a sickening feeling in my stomach by the time I got home that I didn't understand. I was prepared to talk or listen if that's what he wanted.

I tossed my soccer ball in the air for the millionth time. Toss, catch. Toss, catch. Now he was even skipping his oh-so-precious school. I breathed in deeply and counted my breath. I'm not going to get mad.

Suddenly my door slammed open, ricocheting against the wall. I jumped and the ball fell on my face. I shot up, rubbing my forehead and growled, "What the hell, man?"

I raised an eyebrow at him. He was sweaty as if he sprinted from the school to here, and was seething. His hair and eyes were wild. "Nathan..." He gulped air. "He's in trouble."

I stiffened and picked up the soccer ball. Why did he send Marcus? "So?"

"No, you don't get it Ryder. He's in trouble. He's—"

I twitched and turned on him, throwing the ball to him and saying, "It's his life. It's over and you shouldn't care either. We can't do anything unless he comes to us first."

"Ryder—"

"And why should I care, huh? I don't even know what's what anymore. All he does is...is butt into stuff and mess things up. Maybe he deserves-"

He dropped the soccer ball and a second later his fist slammed into my cheek and I fell against the wall. I looked at him in shock, ready to shove him back, but he grabbed the front of my shirt and slammed me against the wall again.

"Deserves? Deserves what?" He yelled. My jaw went slack and still as I stared at my friend. I've never seen him so furious.

"What's wrong with you?!" I half asked, half yelled.

"What's wrong...what's wrong with me? What's wrong with you, Ryder?" He screamed and clenched my shirt with white knuckles. "Do you have any, any, fucking idea what he's going through? What he's been doing these past few weeks? No, no you don't! You have no fucking clue because you sent me to watch over him! So I'm going to tell you. For the past couple weeks he's been working his ass off! All day in the café pretending that he's FINE. As if nothing was wrong with his life. Then when he DOES come to school, he's freaking dead and can't do shit. So what if you got Jonah off his back, he thinks you betrayed him! AND THEN WHAT? All night he serves at a BAR, a freaking bar. Do you know how much he hates alcohol? You don't know what almost happened to him? You sure as hell be thankful I was there to help him! And have you forgotten about that monster asshole he's been paying money to? Well, guess what, he's not waiting for the end of the month anymore. Did you know that? Huh? No. You don't! Want to know how I know that? Because he's lying in his own blood, RIGHT NOW, BARELY able to stay awake!"

He shoved me back and stepped away.

"After all of that, there's you! Do you have any fucking clue how much you hurt him? Nathan has done nothing. He deserves none of this. He deserves to be happy and for a short time, you gave him that. You promised you would never leave his side. And fuck, even I believed you. Who cares what he said or what he did, on top of EVERYTHING he has to handle on his own, YOU were the one that hurt him the most. You were probably the biggest disappointment, and that's why he's giving up. That's why he's not even trying to get back everything he lost."

The look of revulsion never left his face even as he asked, "Where was Nathan at school today?" I could barely comprehend everything Marcus yelled. My mouth opened and closed, unable to speak, as blood drained from my face every second he talked. The part I couldn't get over is that the man Nathan mentioned is still around. He lied about that too? "WHERE WAS HE?" He screamed at me.

"...absent..." I whispered distortedly.

His face twisted and he spat, "And I bet you have no idea where he is."

Chapter ~Thirty-One~

•

"I...I don't understand. No...no, no, no. This can't be happening." I sat back on the bed, staring straight ahead as my thoughts began clouding my mind and I couldn't think straight. "That's not true. It can't be true. Nathan...he...he..." I put a hand over my mouth.

Oh my god.

Oh my fucking god.

"Marcus, tell me you're lying."

His glare was still there and he just looked away. "You had no idea. He lied to you once. That Stevens guy threatened him that if he didn't get rid of you, he would. Everything he's done up till now was for you. And you..." He clenched his eyes shut. "And he begged me not to tell you. He's right. You wouldn't have believed me anyway. You thought he made up the whole thing."

"No...no, I would have. I would have–"

He opened his eyes and glared. "You would have what? That night he came to your house, he was going to tell you everything. And what did you do?" He leaned against the wall. "And now he's alone and hurt, and can't do anything."

I couldn't even think any more. My whole body went cold, my thoughts were a huge mess, and I couldn't comprehend anything. "Where is he...?" I whispered.

"What?"

I am a universal asshole. I should never have waited for him to talk to him to talk to me himself. I should have stayed. I should have watched over him instead of Marcus.

I shot off the bed and grabbed Marcus's shoulders. He gaped, taken aback. "Where is he?!" I yelled frantically.

Oh my god.

"He–"

My ringtone cut him off. I fished out my phone and was about to press end call but Marcus grabbed it and flipped it open.

"What's wrong?"

Confused, I watched him as his face paled. He pulled the phone away from his ear an inch as a high voice shouted through the phone, "HE'S GONE!"

"What do you mean? Where is he? He can't even walk!"

"He's not here Marcus!" The voice sobbed. "He's gone! The door was open when I came back! Marcus, he's not here. Nathan's –"

I couldn't hear anything else. Kristy's voice was completely ignored as Marcus and I just stared at each other. Horror was written all over his face, and I could just imagine what I must have looked like.

We practically flew out of the room. I almost fell down the stairs where mom was waiting obviously worried by all the shouting.

"Ry–"

I let my face show all my emotion I was holding in as I looked at my mom. "Mom, Nathan– I– he– H-he's in trouble and I have to go– I have to– he–"

"Can you call Mr. Kenneth?" Marcus said. "Please, we need help." She nodded, her pale face and we continued our sprint out of my house. We jumped into Marcus's car and he began speeding to Nathan's house. I swear he already ran a stoplight. In the back of my mind I heard a siren and Marcus cuss.

"Your phone is ringing."

"Huh?" I looked down at my phone. It read, Fucker.I answered and growled, "Not now Taylors–"

"Uptown Gardens, Pattson Avenue, number 34." I heard him say a little breathlessly. "That's my house. My uncle said to stay over at a friend's for a while. He said he's dealing with a client."

"If you haven't noticed I'm not your friend and I don't ca–"

"It's Nathan!" He yelled over me, "I know it is. I haven't seen him since earlier this week. My uncle leaves home every night and comes back drunk and fricken gross. Kenneth, he has Nathan. The other day, he referred to him as his client. Marcus's girlfriend is calling every human alive looking for him. I swear if you don't get your sorry ass over there right now and protect your boyfriend, I'm calling NASA...men in black, SOMEONE, that can kick everyone's ass; his and yours! You know, you've been the shittiest jerk I've ever–"

I pressed 'end.' "What was that about?" Marcus glanced at me.

"You know how to get to Gardens, Pattson Avenue?" He nodded slowly. I clenched my teeth and growled, "then hurry."

~~~

.:~* NATHAN *~:.

I blinked slowly. What time was it?

I felt sunlight dancing across my skin, and my eyes shot open.

IM LATE FOR SCHOOL.

I shot up from the covers of a warm bed and immediately caught my breath as pain ripped everywhere. And I mean everywhere. I fell back and curled into a ball.

Oh god. It hurts. My cuts, bruises, head, back, hips, everything. The bed didn't feel warm anymore, it was stuffy. The nice sunlight now felt like cigarette burns on my skin. Outside the sun was still in the sky, but in a couple hours it would set and I would be in darkness, again.

The creak of a door vaguely caught my attention. "Are you up yet?" The rough and teasing voice came closer. "Nathan, wouldn't you rather live here with me? It saves me the trip."

He sat on the bed next to where I lay and stroked my hair.

I shook my head slightly.

He just laughed and leaned very close, "too bad."
~~~

He went to his side of the huge bed, leaning back against his pillows. He motioned with a finger to come to him, but I didn't move. It was too far.

"Come."

I winced and pleaded with my eyes.

"Now."

In the short crawl, I realized I was wearing boxers and a big, thin shirt. Thank goodness.

I lay next to him and for some reason, probably in hopes of distracting myself, I started thinking of the math homework due last week. Yeah, I should do that. Sometime soon. When I get home. Little credit is better than none.

I listened to his irregular heartbeats when he pulled me closer to his side and rubbed his hand along my hurting back. I hope he dies from alcohol poisoning.

Stop it, don't think impossible things.

"You can't go to school anymore," He began saying after a minute of his own relaxation, "One look at you and anybody would be able to tell you sell yourself."

"I've never–"

"And there's no point in working either." I bit my tongue and continued to lay still and extremely tense. "No one will remember you after a month. That sounds good–" He hiccupped. Hiccupped. "–right?"

I nodded.

Suddenly he began laughing. "Finally. You were a hard nut to crack. About time too, that you started listening to me. Isn't it easier?"

I just lay still as he grazed closer to the boxers.

"Nathan!"

His hand stopped moving.

I glanced at the bedroom door a little dumbstruck.

Who was that?

"Nathan!"

My name was heard faintly through the thick walls and doors.

"Who is that?" Mr. Steven asked hollowly. He looked down at me and I literally shot away from him. The look in his eyes, his entire being was angered at the break of his peace. I felt his tipsy attitude turn murderous. "Is that..."

"Nathan! Where are you?"

With my body's aching protest I scrambled backward in the sheets and Mr. Steven narrowed his eyes. "Ryder Kenneth?"

My heart hammered in my chest, for two completely different reasons.

"What is he doing here?"

"I don't know!" He grabbed at me but I kicked at him, suddenly more afraid than I've ever been.

"Why the HELL is your stupid boyfriend–" He grabbed my ankle and yanked me toward him. I tried to kick and pull back but every single motion made something in my body ache and it left me gasping for a second, before attempting to get away again. "I swear! I don't know!"

"NATHAN!" Ryder screamed.

"FUCK, Nathan. Fuck. Damn, fucking SHIT!" He slapped me across my face and I cried into the sheet.

Go away Ryder. Please go away. Just stop it. Please, please, please just–

"I'm coming!"

He sat on top of me and pinned my arms out to the side. He glanced at my left wrist and glared. He grabbed something from beside the bed– a knife.

"Nathan, hold on!"

He raised it above his head and in that moment, I screamed.

I screamed loud and long.

I was scared. Scared to death, like how I was when my dad tried to take me with him, when he ran away from everything he brought on himself, the only way he knew how.

I was going to die. Maybe I deserved it, I did this to myself. But I didn't want to die like this. Like I was still the same useless pathetic child. As if I hadn't fought my whole life. Not now, when I get to hear the voice I've been waiting for so long.

He stuffed it in his belt so he could silence me with a slap on the same cheek, the same cheek he cut hours ago with the bottle, and yelled,"Shut the fuck up! You fucking child. You didn't get rid of him. Do you know what will happen if I am caught? Huh?"

He slapped me again. And again. "If I get sent to jail, wanna know what's gonna happen to him when I get out? Wanna know what I'll do to you?"

There was a pounding on the door. "Nathan?! Was that you? What's going on– was that you? Open the door!"

"You've done it now." Mr. Steven whispered. I just stared back, unable to move or make any indication that I was still comprehending.

There was a loud crash against the door and it rattled threateningly. Again, and again, before finally it slammed open and bounced against the wall.

Ryder's eyes met mine instantly. For some reason, tears fell without my consent. Slowly the tears he hadn't seen for the past week were now visible just for him.

"Get off of him." He said.

"Why should I?" He smirked and purposefully placed a hand on the side of my face. I could practically feel the jab to Ryder as he narrowed his eyes.

Even my shaking steadied for a moment as I stayed as still as possible. I stared back blankly at him. But deep down I was begging Mr. Steven to stop, to not hurt him. And even deeper down, begging myself to believe that if I asked Ryder to save me, he would.

"Tell me, have you gotten this far with him yet?" He chuckled and leaned down, looking at Ryder the whole time he kissed me. Stop it.

"I'll kill you." He swore. "Get the fuck off of him."

He drunkenly laughed at this. "So now you want him huh? Even after he used you just to get some cash–"

"He lied." He interrupted immediately. He looked at only me even though he spoke directly to Mr. Steven, "You were the one that made him do that. He lied. But it doesn't matter. I don't care."

I looked up at Mr. Steven and my heart jumped in my chest. He glared at me threateningly. "Good job, Nathan. You thought you could do something behind my back."

I began shaking my head, "No," I whispered hoarsely, "I told you, I didn't– I swear I did everything–"

He slapped me hard across the face, shutting me up. Ryder shouted, "HEY!" and took a few steps before Mr. Steven shouted, "Move any closer and he's dead!"

He froze immediately, as I realized the metal from his knife was pressed against my throat.

"Stop!" He cried.

I turned my head carefully and whispered in my strained, quiet voice, "Ryder. Get out of here."

He looked at me as if I were the crazy one.

"No..."

"Please, Ry–"

"I'm sorry." He whispered as he let the pain show in his eyes. "I will never leave you by yourself again. I swear."

"Cut the sappy crap." Mr. Steven intervened. He looked at Ryder angrily. "Look kid, Nathan belongs to me. He is my property. Do you get it yet? I don't give a goddamn shit what you think. He is my business, and you should leave. Now."

"No. Never–"

"You want him dead?" He roared. "Because I don't mind! Look!" He grabbed my injured wrist with crusty blood on it. "He tried to do it himself!"

Ryder looked pale, maybe a little sick, but seemingly angrier. If that was possible.

"Lets try something new." He whispered and I felt shivers down my spine. "You let Nathan go, or I take him from your dead hands."

"Ryder, stop–" I said.

Mr. Stevens snickered and simply said, "Fuck you," and reached below my waist.

And then Ryder tackled him.

I felt a huge weight roll off of me as they knocked each other right over the bed, to the floor. Ryder started beating him for dear life with rage written all over his face. I still couldn't move, but I watched with the most surprised (and horrified) face I could muster. Mr. Steven fought back and soon they were both bruised in the face.

I was the only one that could see Mr. Steven grab his knife and push it into Ryders stomach.

He stabbed Ryder.

"Ryder!" I screamed and forced my body to move and shoot forward, shoving him away from Mr. Steven. The latter, who was no longer focused on me whatsoever, pushed me away so I hit my head on the bed frame and grabbed for Ryder, who was a little shocked and dumbfounded as he stared at the place in his side emitting blood.

He hovered above Ryder and shoved the knife again into his side, pulling it out again. He raised it again above his head, and I saw him hesitate, but there was no doubt he would kill him with that knife. He looked just like my dad at that moment, and Ryder had taken my spot.

I refuse.

I don't care anymore. I hate it, I hate it, I hate it. I wont be useless anymore. I wont be a pathetic person that can't do anything to protect something I love. Never, I will never let him be hurt anymore because of me.

I lunged and shoved Mr. Stevens aside and threw myself between the guy I loved and the man I hate. And, for just a second, I felt Ryder's warmth and realized I missed it desperately. I wrapped my arms around and buried my face in his neck, making sure to shield him for the last time, afraid Mr. Steven would rip me away first. I didn't care if I died in a minute, either from what happened in the past week or what was going to happen. I lost too much. I don't want to lose him. Not him too. I refuse. Please let me have just

"Damn you." I heard the person behind me say. "Damn you Nathan."

"I'm sorry." I whispered quietly so only Ryder could hear. I apologized for everything, because I needed to forgive him. And I needed to be forgiven.

"Move!" Ryder shouted and tried to push me away from his body but I didn't let go. "Nathan he–"

I felt the metal-sharp pain pierce my back but I tried not to scream and just clung tighter.

A deafening sound ripped through the air, like a gunshot, angd the weight pressing on the knife disappeared. I noticed Ryder's heartbeat overwhelmed my own, my own heart doing it's best to keep my body runnin. There was screaming but my body went limp and I decided...I could just stay like this. Was Ryder okay?

My grip loosened and I just lay on top of him. There was literally one second of silence before a whole commotion started that I didn't open my eyes to watch.

"Nathan." I heard Ryder's voice say, "Nate! This isn't– this can't happen. Stay awake, please. I love you. I love you so much. Stay with me." Gosh, stop shaking me Ryder. "Nate, I'm so, so sorry. I love you. Na– SOME-ONE HELP HIM! HE'S–"

"I love you too." I whispered. Or at least I think I did. I might've been dreaming already.

And I welcomed the sleep.

I welcomed the dream that reunited me with the only thing that mattered, even if that one thing was screaming his head off.

Chapter ~Thirty-Two~

:~* RYDER *~:.

•

Damn it. Damn everything.

The doctors said "if" he woke up. If.

Why did it come to this? Why only now was Mr. Steven being sent to prison, and being forced to stay there for the rest of his life?

What did Nathan do to deserve this?

I wiped a tear that fell from his face as he slept and held his hand, leaning down till my head touched the bed.

"I'm sorry." I whispered. I felt the tears fall. One by one. "I'm sorry."

I hadn't left his side for the two days since he got out of the ER. Suddenly his head rolled to the side and I glanced up. His face was twisted in pain and his eyes squeezed shut even though he was sleeping. It looked like he was having a nightmare. My heart shuttered and I closed my eyes, making more tears of mine fall onto his palm where I kissed. "It's okay." I whispered. "You're safe. It's okay, everything is okay."

I felt another sob bubble in my throat. It hurt.

His finger twitched and I shot up. All I saw were half opened blue eyes. And I went absolutely still. His eyes were so clear. So vibrant compared to his skin.

He woke up. He woke up! My heart beat wildly as we stared at each other for a full minute. The beating of the monitor increased ever so slightly.

He parted his dry lips. I prepared to hear him tell me to go away, or...or something about the last week. I was ready to answer any questions, reassure him I would never leave him. But in a small, tired whisper, all he said was, "I don't like hospitals."

And I lost it.

"I'm sorry." I cried as tears fell from my eyes, "This whole time, I just– I– I'm sorry." I touched my forehead on his hand, wishing he could just read my mind and understand everything I was sorry for.

I felt him tug his hand away and slowly my heart broke– until he raised it slightly and wiped the tears on my cheek. "This is the first time I've seen you cry...I don't like it." He paused and frowned. "Did you and Marcus finish the project for Math?"

...what?

For some reason in that moment, I realized everything was going to be okay. I don't know why, but that was the moment. I mean, heck! He was thinking about school! But a second later, as he continued saying random stuff, I realized his hands were shaking and he was trying desperately not to cry and lose himself in front of me. He was trying not to face what happened, but everything was coming back to him. And he just didn't want to cry in front of me.

"Nathan." I said quietly. He stopped whispering to himself and looked at me, half afraid. "It's okay." His lips parted and I looked him in the eye, saying, "You don't have to pretend."

After a quiet moment his lip trembled and he squeezed his eyes. He brought his other arm and draped it across his face as he clenched his jaw and tried to keep himself from sobbing. But I saw the first few tears fall down his face and onto his pillow.

"Is it over?" He asked in a voice that shook so much I'm surprised he was able to speak at all.

"Yeah...yeah. It's over." I smiled slightly. "You're safe. It's all over. Kristy shot him and–"

"She what?!" He lifted his arm and looked at me in shock. Oh yeah, I wasn't supposed to tell him that part.

"Marcus got pulled over for his driving on the way to the house. So I ran the last part by myself. He was supposed to get the police, but instead Kristy got both the ambulance and police, and when they got there, I don't know where she got it from but she grabbed one of their stun guns and subdued him long enough for the police to reach us. She shot him right when he...yeah."

He looked at me with huge eyes. "You've got to be kidding m–...KRISTY!" He said loudly and instantly the door shot open and she burst in, pushing me aside rudely and launching herself at his neck where she strangled– I mean, hugged him. He winced and tried to sit up against the head board.

"OH MY GOD, NATHAN!" I pulled her off of him as he tried to breathe and adjust himself.

"Did you steal a gun from a cop and shoot him? That's a crime!"

"What else am I supposed to do?"

"I don't know, wait for the police?"

"Well, at least I know how thankful you are for my quick thinking."

I stared at them as they argued until they stopped in silence. I got a good look at Kristy for the first time and realized she was struggling to keep her cool.

"I–I thought you weren't going to wake up." She said, but a tremble in her voice betrayed her struggling voice. "I was afraid I wouldn't make it in time." Right at the end, her voice broke and she took a big breath as a tear escaped and she blink furiously.

Nathan looked at her in surprise. Then he gave a heart–breaking smile. "Thanks Kristy."

"No problem." She choked out, still trying to remain strong. "You're such an idiot." She hugged him again, gently this time. He closed his eyes and smiled, but something seemed off. Was something bothering him?

"Where's Marcus?"

"In time-out." She said immediately.

He raised an eyebrow. "Time-out?"

"Instead of getting the cops, he went straight to this guys house." She jabbed a thumb at me. "And, he got pulled over by a cop! He didn't have the common sense to not pull over until he got to you, and drag the cop into the house. So as his girlfriend, I have the right to put him in time-out."

"Girlfriend?" I asked in surprise. "So sometime during this whole mess, you and Marcus got together?"

She winked. "Remember that chapter we went to the movies?"

"Chapter 15?"

"Yup."

"Wow."

She leaned to Nathan and kissed the top of his head, and tried to whisper, "Grandma needs to talk to you later," without me hearing. She stood up and faced me. She took a deep breath and whispered fiercely, "I don't care if he forgives you. You make it up to him and he's the happiest gay boy in the world of rainbows."

I nodded quickly, kind of afraid of what she'd do to me if I didn't nod. She smiled at Nathan one last time and backed out of the room, yelling, "MARCUS, HE'S UP! AND WHO SAID YOU COULD LEAVE YOUR SEAT?!"

Finally there was silence.

I looked down at Nathan as he continued to stare at the door where Kristy left. My eyes fell on a boy about my age with black hair sitting in a hospital bed. He turned to me with unsure, blue eyes. The sleeves of his hospital gown ended half way down his arms, and an IV tube was visible where it poked near the new bandages on his wrist. His face was horribly bruised, his neck red. And everything under the gown and blankets were scars that will heal over time, and scars that will never fade.

"I really don't like hospitals." He whispered again. I sat down next to him on the bed and faced him completely. I hugged him. He cringed a bit at the sudden human touch but he didn't pull away.

"It's okay." I said. "This will be the last time."

"Where is he?" He asked in a trembling voice as he closed his eyes.

"Jail." I muttered, "My dad is making sure of it."

"Your dad?"

"He's a lawyer. Don't worry Nate, when my mom told him, he jumped on the case. He wants that guy put away almost as much as all of us."

He was silent for a little bit. "A-are you okay?"

"What do you mean?" I asked as I sat in the chair next to his bed.

"He s-stabbed you, right?"

I pulled away and lifted up my shirt, showing him the gauze wrapped around my torso. "Barely a scratch." Kind of. I wasn't going to give Nate something to feel guilty of. I got out of the ER only an hour after Nathan.

He nodded. I let the peace settle over us for a moment as he stared out the window that was too far for him to see anything.

"Thank you." I said.

He turned his head to look at me with a surprised face.

"The whole time, you were trying to protect me." I clenched my hands in my lap, "And I–"

"I love you."

I looked at him with wide eyes.

He looked a little embarrassed at his words. And scared. And worried. And troubled. As if he was afraid I wouldn't accept him, or I didn't feel the same way.

I leaned in slowly. He began trembling and automatically leaned back. His fear of being touched and being hurt was back. I didn't blame him. I cupped his face and waited until he got used to my touch, then slowly leaned in again and pressed my lips against his. He breathed in through his nose deeply and like the strong person he was, he soon stopped shaking. After a few gentle kisses, he kissed me back.

I wrapped my arms around him and buried my face in his neck, taking in everything about him.

And I thanked every God, real or not, that he was alive.

Chapter ~Thirty-Three~ Final

:~* NATHAN *~:.

●

"What do you mean you did it on your own?" I gasped as Marcus handed a thumb drive with our Math project on it.

"Exactly what I said. I didn't want to bother you and Ryder while you were in the hospital, and Kristy grounded me. I figured I might as well work on it. Who knew if you sit and focus on something, you actually get work done."

"I don't see a problem with it." Ryder smirked as he threw an arm around my shoulders as we walked out of the classroom.

There was a slight hush when we walked down the halls. So much so, that when we stopped at Ryder's locker, Marcus was meeting the eyes of some onlookers.

"Ryder, I think everyone's curious." He muttered.

"Curious of what?"

"Hm, I don't know. It's like you always hang out with Nathan now, as if you like him, or something." He said jokingly.

"But I do like hi– oooh." He glanced around the hall and people pretended not to look. I felt my face warm but kept myself in check. "I don't care. It wasn't exactly a secret to begin with." He looked at me for my thoughts.

Honestly, I wasn't sure how to feel about it. To be...completely honest...my time in the hospital with him by my side was great. And I just wanted to stay by his side everywhere, including school. Oddly, Ryder also freaks out if I leave his side without letting him know. But no one knew he was bisexual, and I didn't want there to be stupid trouble. For him and for me. I should just...give him space at school. Right? No one will be bothered.

"Um...I'm gonna go. I have to turn in all my late work. I'll see you guys later."

"Hey wait, I'll come with yo–"

"It's okay, I have to talk to my teachers too." He looked at me doubtfully but nodded. His hands were clasped tightly.

"Are you gonna watch my soccer practice today?"

I smiled slightly but scolded myself. It's just his practice. No reason to be so happy. "Yeah."

~~

"COME OOOON NATHAN."

"Go away! I said no!"

"BUT I NEED YOU!"

"NO YOU DON'T!"

"WE ALL NEED YOU!"

"ARE YOU KIDDING ME?! YOU SAID I WAS ONLY GOING TO BE WATCHING!"

Ryder wrapped his arms around my waist and dragged me to the soccer field where they were having warm ups.

He wanted me to join the soccer team. And I swear to god, this was frightening.

"Strauss, about time you tried out for my team." Coach nodded in approval.

"Ryder, I can't play soccer. All I know how to do is run." I whispered frantically.

He gave me a small sweet smile and said, "And I'm not as fast as you. We'd make a good pair."

I tugged at the end of my long sleeve. Ryder glanced down at my hands and I stopped immediately. "Fine, but–"

"What is he doing here?"

I looked up and met Jonahs eye as he marched over.

"He's trying out for the team. Got a problem with that?" Ryder said dangerously. Woah, down boy.

"Yes, actually, I do. Tryouts were a month ago."

"Well Coach had asked Nate directly a month ago to join. If you don't like it, you leave."

One by one the other guys on the team were looking over at us. It felt like the day in the mall when they all came and dumped their drinks on me. But this time Ryder was here.

"Unless you want the whole team to quit because of a faggot," He narrowed his eyes, "or two, I suggest you get his and your ass out of here."

Ryder's eyes narrowed slightly. He raised his voice slightly so everyone to hear, "Who doesn't want me here?"

"Me." But after Jonah's response, no one said a word. He looked around him slowly. The guys stared back. "...fucking kidding me..." He muttered. He shoved past Ryder and I and marched off the field.

Then a guy I didn't even know stepped up to me. "Sorry, Strauss. Ryder's our man, so if you join the team, I'm cool with it." The others nodded in agreement.

I took a deep breath. This was weird. This was the most anybody has talked to me in a few years at school. This is the most people I've ever met in one day. And this was the first time I had the option of joining a school sport. But really, I'm mostly considering doing it because it would be good to be a well rounded student on college applications.

I glanced at Ryder. He looked proud of his friends. He caught my eye and smiled.

"Okaaaaay, enough. Come on everyone. You can decide for yourself later, Nathan. Just practice with us today. Or you can referee." Marcus appeared out of nowhere and started pushing us to the center of the field.

~~

I waited for the whole locker room to empty before I changed. Ryder was outside with his friends. I took a look in the mirror.

I still looked kind of ill, but I looked way healthier than I had a week before. I still had bandages all over my torso, and I wasn't supposed to be let out of the hospital. But thanks to Ryder's father that I've come to admire, I'm back in school.

There was a small issue with where I was going. I couldn't live on my own anymore, because Mr. Steven was gone. Apparently, he did have custody over me. Kristy and Ryder had the biggest argument concerning who I was going to live with.

Lets just say it ended with her sock in his mouth, and yelling, "YOU CAN LIVE TOGETHER WHEN YOU'RE MARRIED, HE'S MY BROTH-ER!"

Mrs. Clair and Mrs. Kenneth's conversation seemed just as dangerous. Mrs. Kenneth agreed, saying, "Alright, you can have him for now. But he'll be ours eventually!"

The only condition from Mrs. Clair was that I continue working at Red Rose. With pay. That's all she had to talk to me about.

I've never appreciated the people around me this much. Something swelled in my chest. It kind of hurt. But it made me happy.

"Sorry for interrupting your thoughts, but I needed to talk to you." I jumped and slammed my locker close, swinging around and facing...M attson?

"Mattson?" I asked quietly. I felt guilt wash over me. "Oh god, I'm really so–"

"Hey, look, I don't care. I hated him anyway. He deserves this. I love you more than I remotely liked him."

I felt my face warm. "Mattson, I –"

"Don't worry, I wont do anything. Actually...I have to go. No uncle, no home, no tuition. I'm going back home. But here," He handed me a slip of paper, "If Ryder ever screws up again, I'm one call away. I'm sorry for everything. The asshole's gone, and this is your chance, man. You can do whatever you want. Do what makes you happy."

He leaned in and pecked my cheek. "For the road." He said in his defense. He was halfway out the door but stuck his head back in and said, "Oh yeah, and a little advice. It doesn't matter what other people think. You are who you are, and you like who you like. If someone doesn't like the idea of you with Ryder, they don't matter. You have people who love you. That's all you need. You're strong Nate, stronger than me. Don't let Ryder go. Later, Nathan."

"Bye...Mattson..." and then he left.

I'm strong.

I'm loved.

Don't let Ryder go.

I slowly walked out of the building and looked around for Ryder. There were still a lot of students waiting outside. Finally I saw him by the parking lot. My smile widened and I started walking over.

I stopped mid-step when a few girls jumped up to him and started talking. He nodded shortly and talked, but he really looked bored and uninterested. Suddenly one of them laughed and put a hand on his arm. He politely tried to push her off but she wasn't letting go.

My smile dropped.

I'm strong.

I'm loved.

I may be different, and I may be broken. But that's okay.

Don't let Ryder go.

I started walking again. My strides growing longer and more confident with each step. I stopped right in front of him. I only gave him a second to realize I was there before I moved forward. I focused on him, no one else. I had to tip toe and pull him closer, but that was fine. It was only a small, quick peck on the mouth, but that was fine.

Everything was fine.

He was so stunned it took him a moment to realize what was happening and for him to close his eyes and wrap his arms around me, squeezing me to him.

Don't let him go.

I wont. Not again.

He leaned down again and I smiled against his lips.

I'm glad I'm alive.